Bewitching Amelia

Elia Fairburn

BAD CREATIVE BOOKS

YOU KNOW HOW IT IS. YOU PICK UP A BOOK, flip to the dedication, and find that, once again, the author has dedicated a book to someone else and not you.

Well, not this time.

This one's for you.

I wrote this with you in mind. To entertain, encapsulate, and envelope your mind in my created world for a day or two, or about three to four hours if you're listening to the book.
So, you know what? I'm just going to stop here and let you get on with what fate has destined you to do... Finish this book.

Oh look! A purple rabbit...

This book is a work of fiction. Names, characters, places and incidents are products of the author's imagination or are used fictitiously. Any resemblance to actual events or locales or persons, living or dead, is entirely coincidental.

ISBN 9781691278176

Cover art by Gestvlt

Cover artwork copyright © 2018 by BadCreative

OTHER BADCREATIVE BOOKS

Banking On Love

The Simplest Way To Learn French 2017

The Simplest Way To Learn Spanish 2017

Managing Complications In Anesthesia And Critical Care

Table Of Contents

Chapter One

Provence, France 1927

It was nearing the final curtain of July. The time when the tourist season would see its last few nights of parties and bustling crowds for a while. The French Riviera had proven itself to be much more than everyone had said it would be. Especially, here at the Chateau de la Chèvre D'or. A truly magical place, much like the ones that can only be beheld in paintings that are usually hung in the lounges of people who hope to go there perhaps one day before they die. This place was honestly like something out of a dream, or stolen straight from the stylized vision of something on the movie screen. The vision of a medieval chateau that had been brought back to life in spectacular fashion just in time for the twentieth century. A monument to living lavishly that tethered on a cliff's edge, making it a glorious address for escaping the usual hordes of tourists advancing upon this part of France every year. Giving those lucky enough to be its guests, nothing but a view of the grand, otherworldly, coastal panorama from their hidden cocoon-like terraces and sun decks. A sanctuary where they could lap up the extraordinary and almost supernatural luminosity and colors of the real French Riviera in privacy, one that rivaled that of Adam and Eve.

And, somehow the universe had seen it fit to bless Amelia with the pleasure of visiting this spectacular place in person. She was still not completely sure how or why yet. Maybe the powers that be decided that she get some kind of a break after all of the hell that she had walked through these last few years. Perhaps they felt it was time to show her that there was actually something more to life than getting the rug pulled from under one's feet, even if it was for just a brief moment. Amelia felt that life had finally returned to some form of its former simplicity, where she was concerned in the grand scheme of things. Even though it was just a mere shadow, a silhouette of the simplicity it had once been. She had finally been allowed to return to being a quiet no one, and that is just how she preferred things to be. Living a life in silent solitude, far away from the prying eyes of the bustling crowds. A life eclipsed by the shadow of a flashier and more distracting person. This is why she had decided to take the job with Mrs. Vandemere, her human shield from the poking and prodding world, that only saw her as a source of something to talk about and pity. She couldn't take that anymore, the pity, she got enough of that while she was at home, and that is why she left. Here she was, invisible and getting paid quite handsomely to be so. What more could a girl ask for? Getting to flit around exotic places with all of your expenses paid, and your only requirement is to make someone feel just slightly that they are not alone. Of course, it sometimes required a little more than that, but it was never anything too terribly extreme. A little secretarial work here and there, going shopping, and playing nurse maid to a grown woman who at the slightest sign of people not taking any interest in her being the center of the universe, would suddenly fall ill. Only until you told her that people had been making a fuss about the absence of her presence, of course. This was the only cure. God forbid she were actually to become sick, then no one would believe her.

Amelia lifted her head momentarily to feel the gentle caress of the sun-warmed wind on her delicate and pale cheeks. Mrs. Vandemere had told her she needed to get a little more color so she didn't look like such a ghostly child that someone would find in an old haunted mansion somewhere. The crispness of the sea air filled her nostrils along with the scent of distant fragrant gardens saturated with the aroma of jasmine, roses, and a wealth of various Provencal herbs. The swirling smells and gentleness of the sun that dappled the slowly swaying water beneath her, like a thousand tiny diamonds on aquamarine chiffon, only served to remind her of how different things really were for her now. This was a great departure from the dirty streets of post-world war London, with its gray skies and constant cold rain. No matter what time of the year you found yourself in. Without fail, somehow Mother Nature would find a way to show you that she really could fit all four seasons of the year into one day. But only just as long as you lived in Great Britain, of course. Amelia wondered if there was anywhere else in the world where it was this way. Until now, she had never been any further than Kent, and the thought of even crossing the pond to the states was just a distant fantasy she had held onto as a child. Something she might do with her husband for a holiday one year to impress all of their friends.

When Amelia was much younger, she never imagined at all that this was the way her life would turn out. Not in the slightest. Her life had started out quite modestly, she was born to a somewhat older couple who never expected that they would be blessed with children. This was until one day they miraculously discovered that her mother, Helena, was pregnant with her. A few months later, they moved to the city for her father's job to make a better life for themselves and their new child. Everything was full of promise. Amelia did not remember much about her parents, except that they loved her very much and whatever remained of her memories, as told to her by the people at the group home she was at while awaiting adoption, after the tragic house fire that decimated an entire street. It left her without a family and that ever promising life that she thought she would have.

For most people, not getting adopted while in that sort of situation, usually led to them becoming somewhat unsavory. It was not their fault, and she could not bring herself to blame them. A person must do what they can to survive, but this was not the case for her. The lady that ran the group home always told her that she had a feeling that Amelia was meant for something greater. She could see her moving away and marrying a rich man. Someone who was handsome and deserved her. But she also warned her that life for people who are meant for greatness is never easy. Especially, in the beginning.

In a way, Amelia believed her, at first. But this was until she met Gregory. Gregory was a simple young man. Not in the sense that he was simple minded, no. He was just very 'what you see is what you get', and Amelia admired that about him.

There was no veil over his intentions from the time that she met him. He was very kind, considerate, and honest. Three qualities that would make anyone a good husband, and she was very lucky to have found him, she thought. They fell in love almost immediately. But most importantly, they were friends. She felt as if she could tell him anything and he would be comforting and understanding. He was her rock, and gave her a confidence in herself that she had never known before. The light of her once dreary life. And, this light remained ever so brightly in her life until the year 1914. In July of 1914, her life, and the lives of everyone around her were turned completely upside down, as the country was thrown into war with Germany. Gregory was among the first to be deployed and one of the first to die for his country. He was declared a hero, missing in action. This gave her no peace. Nearly every night for the last thirteen years, she would dream of him still out there somewhere, trying desperately to find his way home to her. But he never came. This drove Amelia to becoming a bit of an agoraphobic. She went for the longest time without leaving the house, to the point that his parents and many of her friends, the ones she had left anyway, were extremely worried about her. There was even talk about her going to stay at a sanitarium. Which is something that she even considered herself. A quiet place where she could just give up on life, because there was no reason to live it anymore. Gregory was no longer there, so what was the point. The light in her life had been completely snuffed out, never to return again, except in now occasional and fading nightmares. She did her best to cling to them, for they were the only thing she had left of him now. Amelia could not bear to be parted with them. Even though she knew eventually that they too would leave her and she would be left with no more traces of his fading memory.

Amelia was quite surprised at herself for even taking this job, really. She, even now, could not figure out what exactly had possessed her to become Mrs. Vandemere's companion. She wondered if it could have possibly been the fact that people told her it would give her purpose. Or perhaps it was the idea of traveling to places she had never been to or seen before, unless she happened to be looking at picture post cards in some corner shop somewhere. Now she was there. But still all she could think about was Gregory. She imagined how much he would have loved this place. Amelia felt half tempted to write him a letter as if he were still alive, and tell him about everything that she was doing now. How would she begin, though?

I am just writing to you from the terrace. I have just had my breakfast in companionship with a lovely view of the sea. It is exactly the paradise you told me about; the people are delightful, the sun is warm but not too unpleasant. Yesterday afternoon, when I arrived here, I could have sunbathed...

Amelia stopped short and the voice in her mind faded away with the wind, as she felt a heaviness grow in her chest. The tears creating a mist in her eyes, like the one she had witnessed over the top of the sea earlier that morning. She shook her head under her humble straw beach hat that covered her uncommonly long blonde hair. It was unusually long for someone of her age these days, she had been told. Everyone told her that she should get a bob, they were all the rage now. Only little girls had long hair nowadays. It told the world that you had moved into sophisticated womanhood when you got a haircut, and that you had officially made your move into the height of stylish society. But Amelia had no real reason now to have any major concerns for her appearance. She preferred to wear clothing that was comfortable and functional, rather than worrying about impressing anyone. In fact, she much liked the fact that the mousy grays, dull browns, and beiges that she wore afforded her quite a different quality. Invisibility. This way, she could go through the rest of her life in the background, unnoticed and unbothered by other members of society. It was not that she had anything against them. She just much preferred not to worry herself with the small or great concerns that were harbored by most people in the human race now. If she could completely disappear altogether and spend the rest of her days in a bed somewhere in a dark room, she would. But alas, this apparently was not something that a functioning member of the human race was meant to think. What they did not realize was that she was only a relatively functioning member of humanity now, and she feared that there was no way to reverse it.

The only thing that gave any kind of inclination to anyone that there was a flicker of life remaining in her body, was that she very much enjoyed sketching. It was very therapeutic to her, because she did not have to think very much when she did it. Amelia could just sit outside, very much like she was doing now, and let her hand guide her pencil over her sketch pad. The only thing she had to do then was wait to see what it would come up with today. And today, her hand felt the desire to capture the image of a small sail boat, as it glided towards the sinking evening sun.

Suddenly, there was the sound of a low roar on the beach above her. Rocks cast themselves from the small, naturally crafted rampart and skipped their way down to her, in indication that something had disturbed them. Amelia cast her eyes up briefly to see what they were trying to show her. And, that is when she saw him. There he stood, a tall, ominous figure of a man. Despite the warmth of the day, he wore a long dark trench coat. His hair was black and his skin pale. He much reminded her of one of those figures from a horror movie she had gone to see with Mrs. Vandemere. A vampire. From where she sat, his eyes looked almost as black as his hair. It could have been a trick of the light. Or was it something more? Amelia could not be sure. There was something about him that was foreboding yet enticing. Something she could not quite put her finger on. Who was he? And, what did he have in store for her? The questions that flooded her mind confused her. What did he have to do with her anyway? She had never seen him before in all of her life. Yet somehow, she felt that she had. Whatever was about to happen already had somehow. It was fated.

Amelia quickly cast her eyes back down in deep concentration onto the sketch pad, hoping that he would not notice her as she had noticed him. Perhaps, if she stared down at the paper long enough, not only would this overwhelming feeling of premonition leave her, but so would he.

Amelia slowly raised her head and peered out from under the now low-hanging brim of her straw hat. It worked, she thought to herself, with a sigh of relief. Both he and the car had vanished just as quickly as they had arrived, and she was now safe. Once again, she was completely alone.

Chapter 2

The lights in the grand dining room of the Chateau de la Chèvre D'or were so bright they were nearly blinding. It felt as if it were still daylight somehow, though the guests were all inside. And, just as the outside of the great structure had been updated to match the opulence and splendor of these new times, so had the interior. A grand orgy of evidence that if you were a world traveling sort of person with lots of money to burn, they would prefer you come burn it here. Or rather eat and drink it here.

Amelia found herself sitting as she usually did these days, around this time, at a table much too large for two people with her employer and constant companion, Mrs. Vandemere. A lady of nearly sixty, who feels the need to play the part of mutton dressed as lamb to the fullest extent possible. A look complete with a loud, low-cut blazing red dress and a frizzy bottle red bob that she says was to match, but clearly that was not the case. And, Amelia feared that she would surely get a migraine if she continued to look at her under these harsh lights, which only served to accentuate every crag and wrinkle that her once beautiful skin now possessed. Amelia only hoped that she would never find herself succumbing to the same fate that this poor woman seemed to be doomed to. The fate of spending the rest of her life going to exotic places, to hunt down wealthy widowers and divorcees unfortunate enough to make their way into the clutches of her spider's web. Only to be tossed away at some later date, after she had drained them of all of their money. A woman has to make a living somehow, she quipped to herself. And, as long as the Misses has some kind of income so would she, until such a time as the old bat was no longer kicking, of course. Hopefully, that would be quite some time from now. But with a woman of her age and reputation, one could never be sure. Amelia was sure, however, that there would be others after, though. So, she would not have to worry too much about finding work. Especially, in a place like this.

Mrs. Vandemere sighed loudly and puckered out her bottom lip. "What's happened to this place? Hmm? Do you think the management will give me a discount?" She complains. "I mean, what do they think I come here for, to look at waiters and bellhops? Though, I will have to say that one is pretty cute." She leered in the direction of some young waiter in a gray uniform, that was far too form fitting for Amelia's taste.

Amelia looked down at her scattered seafood salad. She had only had the appetite to chase it around her plate, while averting her eyes from the nicely crafted behind of the young man Mrs. Vandemere was admiring so intently. She could feel her cheeks becoming flushed and red. Closing her eyes, Amelia tried to concentrate on the taste of the bite she had just put in her mouth. Hopefully, that would cool down the flames she felt rising into the skin of her face.

"Once upon a time, maybe if I was a few years younger." Mrs. Vandemere continued. "Or perhaps not, you know how boys seem to have a thing about women who are old enough to be their mother."

Amelia suddenly dropped her fork. It clanged much louder than she anticipated as it made contact with her plate, startling her even further. Her eyes felt as if they were about to leap from their sockets. She could not believe that Mrs. Vandemere would say such a thing, especially in a public place where other people could hear her. Did this woman really possess so little tact?

Mrs. Vandemere returned her strange expression with a sly smile and asked, "What, dear? Are you shocked? Well, of course you are." She laughed as she went back to shoving shrimp into the open, awaiting chasm of her horse teeth filled mouth. Amelia stared uncomfortably as the sound of squishing and moist squeaking filled her ears, causing her to shudder with disgust.

Amelia looked down once again, trying her very best to be invisible. So invisible even, that maybe Mrs. Vandemere would forget that she was there altogether and stop talking to her for the rest of the evening. If only Mrs. Vandemere would see somebody she knows and ask them to join them, Amelia found herself praying silently. At least that way, there would be some kind of a buffer between her and this terribly crass woman she had, for whatever reason, chained herself to.

Just then, while still stuffing her face, Mrs. Vandemere's attention was abruptly stolen away momentarily by someone entering the dining room. Amelia felt amazed at the fact that her prayer was answered quite so quickly. She must have been putting forth a lot more feeling than she anticipated. If only this sort of thing worked when she asked for large sums of money to be falling from the sky. Or for herself to disappear completely from the face of the earth. Oh well, for now she would have to be satisfied with this.

Mrs. Vandemere hurriedly snatched up her pince-nez from out of her bosom and opened them with a loud, one handed snap. Peering through them with beady squinted eyes, she said, "Now wait a minute, here is somebody. A real somebody, and how." She gasped suddenly, as though amazed to even see them in a place like this. "It's Septimus Creede. He is the last living owner of Creede Castle. You have heard of, Creede Castle, haven't you?" She violently patted

Amelia's arm in giddy excitement, as she pulled her compact from her clutch to fluff her hair and check the rest of her appearance. Reaching into the small hand bag, she retrieved a card and her eyeliner pencil. Then, quickly scribbled what appeared to be an almost unintelligible note.

"Of course," Amelia acknowledged quietly, as she looked up, suddenly realizing that he is the very same man that she saw out on the beach only a few hours earlier that day. Picking up her glass of wine, she buried her nose in it, hoping that he wouldn't notice her. She couldn't be sure if he saw her earlier as well. Hopefully, he didn't then, and he wouldn't now.

"He's been ill, you know?" Mrs. Vandemere rattled on. "They say that he can't get over his wife's death. She supposedly drowned in the bay near the castle. So very tragic, isn't it?" She let out a forlorn and sympathetic sigh. Amelia was sure it was loud enough for everyone within a hundred miles to hear, and most likely the volume was deliberate.

Mrs. Vandemere clanged loudly on her wine glass to get a nearby waiter's attention. The same young man she had been leering at only moments before swiftly came to her side. Slowly, she slowly handed him the note and said, "Here, take this to the gentleman over there sitting alone, with the Maitre D."

Digging an undoubtably moist bill from her breast with two fingers, she slipped it to the young man, who did his best to refrain from looking on her with fear and disgust. "If you do it quickly, there is more where that came from."

Amelia buried herself further into her glass of wine, hoping that somehow it would allow her shrink in size and drown her. This was perhaps the only way to save her from enduring the inevitably embarrassing events that were about to occur. She needed to find some way to escape, but she couldn't think of anything. Yet, somehow it was like a train wreck that she couldn't look away from, she was simply frozen; watching almost in slow motion as the waiter brought him the note. Amelia cringed heavily, feeling the sliminess of the discomfort crawl over her skin, as she saw him look in their direction and the waiter pointing to where the note came from. Suddenly, she got the urge to run over to him and get on her knees to beg his forgiveness. Also, to deny any involvement that she had in it. But he simply looked at her with a slight glint in his eyes. A glimmer that quickly brought a flush to her cheeks and a smile to her lips, which she didn't understand at all. What was this feeling that he had suddenly inspired within her? It was magnetic, like some kind of vacuum that she couldn't explain. It was as if all of a sudden, they were the only two people in the room, and all time and space had ceased to exist around them.

However, this feeling was short lived. So short lived that there was really no time for her to inspect it any further because of the great talent Mrs. Vandemere had for crashing into situations like a wrecking ball. "Persephone," Amelia's thoughts were quickly shattered by the sound of her employer's voice. "That is what they called her, his wife, that is. She was a real beauty." Mrs. Vandemere admired herself once again in her compact, before casting a quick side glance towards Amelia. "But then again, weren't we all at one time." She winked, snapping the compact shut and smiling in Septimus's direction.

Amelia sat there on the expansive settee that seemed much too small because of the company that shared it. Everywhere they went, her employer's personality made up more than the difference for what she lacked in size. Causing everyone around her to feel claustrophobic no matter how far away they were sitting from her. Particularly, Amelia and especially just now as they were seated across from the intimidating figure of Mr. Septimus Creede. And, it didn't help that it felt as if he was staring straight into her soul with his unwavering and piercing glance. When, all she wanted to do was melt into a puddle and run away. However, there was something about him that she just couldn't seem to shake. If only Mrs. Vandemere would stop talking for the better part of five seconds, she could probably figure it out and just as quickly forget about it. But, of course, as luck would have it, she continued.

"It is really so good of you to join us. You know, I did wonder just that little bit if you would remember me."

"Immediately, Mrs. Vandemere. Exactly where?" He asked politely, but with the undertone that he was barely tolerating her for the purpose of pursuing something else entirely.

"My cousin Millie's birthday, at Clarages." Mrs. Vandemere tried to jog his memory.

"Oh," he replied as if unsure, but he was going to go along with it.

"But I'll tell you he was so proud to have you as his friend. Oh, and the way he talked...gushed really about Creede Castle, with stars in his eyes. Like he had been to some fairy land. I do wonder how you can bear to ever leave it. Millie said that...that galleried hall, he said it was a gem. I'll bet that castle has entertained royalty, eh?" she rattled on, not allowing Septimus to get a word in. He kept looking to Amelia as if he wished she would say something to break the flow of nonsense coming from Mrs. Vandemere's mouth.

"To be honest, the castle has not entertained the likes of royalty since Ethelred, the one they called the unready. Everyone said it had something to do with the fact that he was always late to everything, especially dinner. But I always got the impression it had something to do with how he was never known to have much sexual prowess."

Mrs. Vandemere laughed heartily, slapping Amelia on the arm and shaking her. Amelia was shocked at herself for also feeling a smile creeping onto her face, and feeling tempted to laugh, even though she usually found that she was customarily quite shocked by such a subject matter. What was it about him that made it so different for her?

"You don't really seem to know many other people here this season, you should take the time to come up to the suite some time. Maybe we could organize a little party. Only the who's who of course, that is if we can find anyone..." Mrs. Vandemere began, as she pulled a cigarette that couldn't have been any shorter than a one twenty from her overly case and shoved it onto the end of her extra-long holder. The length of the two combined made her look like some sort of over exaggerated caricature, from some newspaper comic strip. Amelia tried to hold in her laughter at how ridiculous it was, that Septimus almost did not have to reach out from his side of the table, to play the part of the perfect gentleman and light it for her.

"I'm afraid not, I have only just arrived, and as you say I don't know anyone here." He declined, before suddenly turning his attention completely on Amelia. The force of his magnetism as strong as if he had grasped her face with his hand and purposefully made her look deep into his eyes. "What do you think of Provence?"

Amelia did her best to recover from the sudden shock of finding that he was actually speaking to her, and began to answer his question, but as soon as she opened her mouth to express her thoughts, she was abruptly interrupted by her employer.

"She really is very spoiled, you know. Because, most girls her age would give their eyes just to get a glimpse of this place." Mrs. Vandemere declared.

"That would rather defeat the purpose, wouldn't you say?" Added Septimus, dryly.

Mrs. Vandemere let out a shrill cackle and began to choke on the smoke of her cigarette. It did not bother Amelia, however, as it usually did; making her feel uncomfortable or embarrassed. For her mind was too occupied with thoughts of the man across from her, and the warmth of the humorous feeling that was now shared between them. She felt as if they were two old friends now sharing an inside joke between one another at the old foolish woman's expense.

Later that night, as Amelia sat up in her bed. She was finding it quite difficult to sleep. This wasn't something completely unusual for her. Since the death of her husband, sleep did not come to her very easily anymore. So, she had taken up the practice of finding things to occupy herself with, until such a time as her body became too exhausted to keep up the battle, and finally allow her to drift into the land of dreams. A land that had also been laid barren to her since the death of her beloved, and she figured this was probably why she found that she had less enthusiasm for sleeping, because there was no longer anything awaiting her on the other side of the veil that lies between asleep and awake.

Tonight, she sat with her back against the oak headboard of the single bed that stood next to a humble night table, where a solitary lamp gave off a meager amount of light. It was enough for Amelia to see the new addition she was rapidly and attentively adding to the collection of various works of art in her sketch pad. This one however, was very different from all the rest. It was unlike anything you would usually find within her many books, which were filled to the covers with depictions of still life's and landscapes of flowers, and birds or other woodland creatures. This was a portrait. The portrait of a dark and mysterious man, with sharp features and piercing perceptive eyes that even from within the page penetrated her soul, and beckoned her to be his. And strangely enough, she found herself wanting to surrender to the pull of his desire. Like the great draw of the homing beacon that lives within all nature, drawing it back to the places of their origin. The siren song that ultimately calls them all back home. Home. The place that the universe fated them to belong to and to which there was no altering of, no matter how much one tries to fight it. What was it about Septimus that inspired such feelings in her? Feelings that she was sure had died all those years ago. She had been so sure that the scorched earth of her soul would never be able to allow love bloom there ever again. Until now, causing her to wonder if she had been wrong about this, what else was she mistaken about?

Chapter 3

The very next morning, Amelia set out on her own. Everything seemed to be covered by a new and brighter lens. The sea seemed more spectacular, the flowers more fragrant, and the sun warmer and more illuminating. Amelia was not sure if it was the fact that she was experiencing the gentle caress of love in her heart once again, or if it was that Mrs. Vandemere would be confined to her room today under no uncertain terms. She had informed Amelia that apparently, she did not feel very well. Amelia knew better though. This was just her way of having her own personal pity party, for the clear fact that she hardly ever felt there were enough people paying her enough attention, to make her feel like the center of the universe. This meant that she would most likely be spending the better part of the next few hours or maybe even days in bed. It all depended on whether she would become bored of spending quite so much time in her own company sooner rather than later. Either way Amelia did not care. This meant that she would finally be able to enjoy something that had become a somewhat foreign concept to her since becoming Mrs. Vandemere's companion. Peace and quiet.

Walking out onto the vast terrace of the hotel, she took no notice of the mostly occupied tables of various patrons having their morning meals, or just simply reading the paper and drinking coffee. Stepping to the edge of the terrace, Amelia lifted her face to the sun. Closing her eyes, she took in a deep cleansing breath, filling her nostrils and lungs with fresh, spritely sea air. The sound of the people's chatter being drowned out by the peaceful breeze, rustling through the branches of the rose bushes like the quiet whispers of small cherubs, and promising her that today was going to be a good day.

"Good morning," a deep, manly voice suddenly came into her ear and she turned with a start to find Septimus standing next to her.

"Oh, good morning," she replied with a quiet smile.

"I see you are alone." He said.

"Um, yes, yes I am." She replied.

"Come join me," Septimus invited her with a wave of his hand and Amelia felt somehow as if she could not refuse.

Making their way to a small table, he pulled out a chair for her and allowed her to sit before taking a seat himself across from her, where he looked at her with gleaming eyes, and a bright smile that reminded her very much of a cat. A cat that was all too pleased with itself for catching a canary. Amelia smiled and looked down, feeling a flush come to her cheeks as she noticed herself becoming embarrassed. She wasn't quite sure why he was looking at her in such a manner.

"I'm sorry for being so rude last night," he said finally, breaking the awkward silence.

"Oh, but you weren't." She assured him.

"Not to you perhaps. How is your friend?"

"She has come down with what she calls a touch of influenza." Amelia said laughingly.

With an expression of feigned sympathy, he responded, "to be treated with copious amounts of champagne cocktails I suspect." This caused Amelia to believe that he was just as perceptive as he appeared. Though, it really wouldn't take anyone with the intellect of Sherlock Holmes to decipher just what kind of a person her employer was.

With a snap of his fingers, he summoned the waiter on the other side of the terrace. Without even flitting his eyes away from hers for a second he said, "Garson, we will have poached eggs, toast with marmalade, sausage, a tomato, and tea. Yes?" Septimus nodded at her to confirm. To which she nodded back fervently. It had been so very long since she had had a full English breakfast, since she had begun traveling about Europe with her American employer. And she had missed it very much. Who was this man that seemed to know her every whim?
Amelia stopped herself before her thoughts took her too far. Despite the fact that his attention made her even happier than she felt she ever had been, she knew that she did not

need to overthink this. For that would be the fastest track to heart break, she was sure of it. So, she decided that it would be best to just savor the moment. Enjoy and savor every second of it, and let the universe gradually show her what it had in store for them, and allow herself to be pleasantly surprised.

A short while after breakfast, Septimus offered to take Amelia on a tour of the grounds of the hotel. And since she did not really have anything else to do, she accepted. Even though Amelia never really thought of herself as one who had the gift of gab, she found it very easy to speak to him. It was as if the words just flowed from her, and before she knew it, she had pretty much told him her entire life story. But he never seemed to tire or become bored of her as she spoke. He listened just as intently as when she began.

"So, you see, this is why Mrs. Vandemere decided to take me in and teach me to be a paid companion." She continued.

"I was not aware that someone could buy friendship." He commented, after having been silent up until now.

"Well, not the real sort of friendship, no. You know I looked up the word companion in the dictionary once, and it said that companion means, to be a friend of the bosom."

Septimus threw his head back and laughed heartily. "Oh, my. So, do you not have any family at all?"

"Not since my parents, but as I told you, they died when I was but a child." She paused for a moment, feeling suddenly pulled to tell him one more truth about herself that she had kept hidden until now. But if things were to go on, he should know, she thought to herself. She thought it strange that she somehow felt she had the strength to actually utter the words without bursting into tears, unlike so many times previous.

"Especially, not since my husband passed away some thirteen years ago, in the war. We were married very young, and very briefly. It wasn't long after that, that he was deployed here to Europe and went missing in action. Since I have been here, I keep thinking that somehow, I will run into him as some poor vagrant on the side of the road who has lost his memory, or that he is desperately trying to find his way home to me. But it has been too long now to hold on to any kind of hope any longer." Her voice trailed off as she watched Septimus's face suddenly change, afraid that she had somehow said something that would no longer make her attractive to him. Then, his features softened.

"We both have something in common then, we are both truly alone in the world. Essentially. Except, I still have a sister and an ancient grandmother. But neither of them really keep me company, because that would require them to live with me and honestly I don't think that would work out very well."

"At least you do have a place you can call home though. That must be some consolation. Somewhere you can call your own. You know, I once bought a picture post card of Creede Castle when I was a child, cost me half of my pocket money." They shared a laugh. Septimus smiled warmly before his expression drifted into an empty and almost sad look of longing. He looked away over to the sea, his gaze staring far and thoughtfully into the middle distance. "Some home it is. Just a big, empty house that sometimes can be as lonely as a crowded hotel." He continued to look away, before suddenly re-centering his eyes upon her.

"So, what is going to happen to you when Mrs. Vandemere has one too many of those cocktails she enjoys so much, and takes a tumble down the stairs, snapping her expensive neck?" He asked, shuffling the stones at his feet like a school boy, with his hands casually in his pockets.

"I suppose there will be others." She found that she much liked this side of him. Softer, gentler. She felt much like someone who had gained the trust of a wild and dangerous animal.

"Plenty, and for one so young as you, life holds no terrace for you does it? I'm twice your age, you know..." he paused for a moment and stroked back a lock of her uncommonly long hair. Amelia prepared herself for what she feared might happen. The anticipation grew inside of her as she wanted and waited for him to kiss her.

"Go put on a hat," Septimus instructed, brushing her cheek gently before walking away.

It wasn't long before Amelia found herself sitting in the passenger seat of his car, flying down one of the coastal roads. "There is really quite a spectacular view of the sea that can be seen from the windows of Creede Castle. Even though, I will have to say it is a bit different than it is here in the Riviera. It's a bit colder and grayer, much like the entire place. Like something out of a gothic novel. Unless of course you are there in the spring time. Then, is when it is at its most beautiful, a lively and colorful place covered in every variety of wild flowers that you can possibly think of, and probably even some that you can't. The grounds are quite vast, so it would take you sometime to see all of it. You know, I have always thought that wild flowers are meant to be left in nature. This is why I never allowed anyone to pick them and bring them into the house. Such vandalism, don't you agree? My sister always complained about always feeling drunk from the strong aroma of the place. I never could understand how that would be something to complain about. It's the only kind of drunkenness I like. There is nothing like the feeling of crushing a handful of petals in your hand and a thousand scents come rushing into your head." As he said this, Amelia watched as his face changed without warning to that of a man who had seen a ghost. His eyes grew wide in a frightened hypnotic trance, and all of the color seemingly began to drain out of not only his face, but his entire body. Turning her gaze once more to the road, she realized that it was rapidly running out, and they were headed straight for the edge with a long drop off into the sea. His foot lay heavy like a dead weight on the gas pedal, pushing them ever faster towards what would ultimately be their certain death. She screamed in terror, covering her eyes and feeling the ends of her nails claw into the skin of her face.

Septimus shook his head and blinked his eyes, awakening to reality once again. Taking quick action, he stamped his foot on the brake and forcefully swerved the car to a screeching halt, with dust flying through the air around them as rocks skipped down the ravine. Amelia listened for them, taking notice of how long it took them to make it to the surface of the rock-strewn face of the turbulent water. She now knew it must be several feet below. All she could think of now was the sound of her own shallow and ragged breathing, burning with every terrified inhale.

Septimus placed his hand on her arm. She flinched, still in shock. "I'm sorry, Amelia. Please forgive, even though I know that was unforgivable of me."

"Can we please go back now?" She answered in a hoarse whisper.

A gripping fear saturated Septimus eyes and washed over his face. Amelia got the sensation that somehow his fear, however, did not stem from their recent and sudden brush with death. There was more to it, something deeper. His eyes scanned her face over and over, as if to ask if she had lost all trust in him, and they pleaded desperately for the answer to be an emphatic, no. Amelia let out a gentle exhale and did her best to soften the severity of her appearance. Curling a slight smile on her small, delicately pink lips, she felt this to be the best and only way to assure him that everything was all right. And that he did not have to fear any longer that she would suddenly bolt from the car and run frantically down the road, never to see or speak to him ever again. She watched as he began to relax, and his face took on a bit of a smile itself, however cautious. He seemed to finally be recovering.

Septimus put the car back in drive and began to make his way back onto the road. Pulling over to the edge of the ravine slowly, he brought the metal beast to a stop. He leaned over her, directing her also to look down into the drop. "It really is not so bad after all. "

"No... No, I suppose it isn't. "She replied slowly.

Septimus reached over and took her by the hand, giving her small, delicate hand a slight squeeze, as a way to assure her that as long as he was there, she would not want for protection. Just then, he reached into the backseat and retrieved a large pair of driving gloves.

"Here, put these on, your hands are cold. This will take care of that. "

"Thank you, "Amelia obliged, at a loss to say anything else. Putting them on, she realized just how very large his hands were in comparison to hers. And for reasons that she was completely uncertain of, the over exaggerated appearance of the gloves made her feel very comical. She suddenly got the image of a carnival clown wearing large shoes in her mind's eye, and this made her start to laugh uncontrollably. Before long he had joined her, and they sat there for several minutes laughing, rather than crying over the harrowing experience they had both shared.

Amelia took a deep breath and wiped the tears of laughter and fear from her eyes. Taking a moment, she looked around at the scene around them that had become more peaceful.

"You must know this place very well." Amelia observed.

"Yes, that isn't very difficult, for it doesn't change much with time; that's for certain."

Amelia got the distinct impression that he was alluding to something else he did not feel was yet safe to tell her. And in that moment, she wondered if there would ever come a time if he would. What was it about this place that affected him so badly? She only knew that it could be a great number of things. His first wife, the war, but she found that she was too afraid to ask at this point. It was too early, and she would be content to just be patient and allow him to tell her in his own time; if that day would ever come.

"Come along, milady, I'll see you back now."

Amelia felt the tug of reluctance as he pulled away and onto the road once again, not wanting this moment to end. But she knew deep in her heart that if he had anything to say about it, this would not be the last of moments like these, most likely for the rest of her life.

Upon returning to the hotel, Amelia bid Septimus farewell, because he told her that "good-bye" is something that people say to each other when they plan on never seeing one another ever again. And he had plans to meet her again tomorrow, that is if she was not too frightened of his driving. To which she giggled like a silly school girl, and assured him that she would like that very much. So it was set. There was just one thing she had to be certain would not get in the way of their well laid plans. In the bliss of her outing with Septimus, where she felt that they were the only two people on the face of the earth, she had completely forgotten about Mrs. Vandemere.

Amelia tentatively opened the door leading into Mrs. Vandemere's suite. She feared that she would find her suddenly recovered and it would dash any hope she had of seeing Septimus alone tomorrow. However, upon opening the door, all of her fears were immediately eased by the sight of her employer still lounging in the bed.

At hearing someone come in, Mrs. Vandemere sat up quickly and pulled up one side of her pink, ruffled, blind fold to see who had entered her bedroom.

"Oh, there you are, girl." Mrs. Vandemere declared. "Where were you off to all day?"

Amelia smiled as she came closer to the side of the bed. She poured water out of the carafe and into a glass which she handed to Mrs. Vandemere. Realizing the brightness of her beaming expression, she did her best to quickly squelch it for fear that the lady would catch on to what she had been doing. Amelia could not tell her. Her time with Septimus was too sacred, too precious, to share with the likes of someone like her.

"What have you been up to?" Mrs. Vandemere asked in a sly tone, letting Amelia know that she had not been quick enough and she had caught a glimmer of something. Amelia knew that if she did not cut her off at the pass, she would surely vacuum it out. Mrs. Vandemere was like a shark when it came to collecting juicy details. Once she smelled the slightest trace of blood, there would be no way to get her to let go until she got everything she desired and more.

"Oh, I decided to try something new and play a little tennis with one of the instructors today." Amelia lied, hoping this would be enough to convince her. If all else failed she could try and change the subject to the lady herself, for she never missed an opportunity to elaborate about herself to an audience. Even if it was only an audience of one. Poor, sad, lonely woman that she truly was.

"Well, my dear, whatever he did for your back hand certainly put some color in your cheeks. Maybe, I need to get some of those kinds of lessons, too." Mrs. Vandemere winked and smiled like a prowling wolf, before downing a fistful of what Amelia could guess to be pain killers, and chasing them with the last of her champagne cocktail. She smiled behind her hand as she thought of how exactly Septimus had pegged Mrs. Vandemere, right down to the last obscure detail.

"So did you see anyone new? Did anyone relatively distinguished arrive at all today? Anyone ask about me?" Mrs. Vandemere asked, her words filled with anxious anticipation.

"No, I'm afraid not. It was all pretty much the same as yesterday and the day before." Amelia said solemnly, feeling slightly guilty for bursting the poor woman's bubble, in hopes that it would buy her more time to do what she desired to do instead, without the worry of babysitting her all day. But she couldn't help herself, she needed to be with him. She needed to wring every moment with him out of this trip that she possibly could, knowing that at any time Mrs. Vandemere could suddenly desire to leave for some other far away destination and she would have to fulfill her obligation; putting her in danger of never seeing him ever again. That being said, if causing the woman to wallow in bed for the next few days was the price she needed to pay, to be able to savor every last second, it was well worth it. She thought to herself.

Mrs. Vandemere pouted loudly, and picked up the mirror that sat on her small, bed top tray table. Running her hands over her clean, make-up free face, she gave herself a disgusting look of disappointment; as if to tell herself she needed to do better. "You know, I think I really should send for a doctor. From the looks of things, I think I am really getting worse." Mrs. Vandemere surmised, as she continued to look at herself and stick out her tongue in the mirror.

Finally, after reaching the highest level of displeasure with her own appearance, she pounded the small mirror down on the top of the tray table, face down. "Uggh!" She laid back and let out a whine, like that of a small child who has just been told that they cannot have what they wanted. Suddenly, and almost as though she had had some kind of epiphany, she pulled herself out of this distraught like state and eagerly asked, "Did you see Septimus today?"

Amelia was taken aback by this, her mind reeling and scrambling as she tried to figure out the best way to tell her. But she couldn't quite bring herself to lie again. "Well..." she began.

"Yes, yes, well, what? Did you see him or not?" Mrs. Vandemere urged, rolling her hand like someone would a roll of cinematic film.

"I saw him at breakfast this morning," Amelia stated, internally patting herself on the back for finally finding an intelligible sentence.

"Oh, really? You say you saw him, meaning he was alone. Did he have lunch with anyone?" Mrs. Vandemere pried further.

"He wasn't in the restaurant at lunch time." Amelia finally felt like she was getting the hang of this game of strategic verbal cat and mouse.

"Ah ha, there you are! See!" Mrs. Vandemere uttered, triumphantly wagging her long, aged finger in the air like she had locked onto something significant. "They say he never mentions her name. He just won't talk about it, or let anyone get near him. You see how he just brushed me off."

Amelia smiled quietly to herself, once again, and began to wonder what it was about herself that made him think her so special, that he would allow her to come into the inner sanctum.

"I don't see why I shouldn't take another crack at it." Mrs. Vandemere picked up the mirror again and began to pinch her cheeks to bring color to her face, as she primped in her reflection. "Just let me get back up on my toes again, I think Septimus Creede is far too good a man to turn a lady down twice; even if she is not that much of a lady."

Chapter 4

Luckily for Amelia, Mrs. Vandemere did not find the stamina to get back up on her toes quite as quickly as she would have liked. So the next couple of days were filled with an array of various adventures. She felt almost as if Septimus was showing her the world for the first time. Taking her driving around the coast, picnics in a secluded meadow, swimming in the ocean; where she was finally able to behold just how beautiful of a man he truly was. Often finding herself utterly overwhelmed by the sight of his great stature and broad, barrel chest and formidable shoulders. Quite an intimidating figure of a man, unless of course you were lucky enough to be her, and were allowed to see just how soft and gentle of a person he was deep down. His piercing dark eyes that were normally so stern and stormy, all calm and warm in the way they looked at her. She wondered if this is what they meant by the term, worship. She couldn't help but feel at times that he was indeed worshipping her. And, the feeling was certainly mutual, for many times she caught herself just staring at him. But he never called her out on it or made her feel uncomfortable for doing so.

After a long morning that had really not seemed that long, they decided to break their day of excursions about Provence, by stopping off at a small, outdoor cafe. Amelia sat across from him, where she once again found herself staring thoughtfully into his eyes. She felt words begin to make their way into her mouth, but she decided to keep the thought to herself, for fear that she would sound silly or childish.

"What were you going to say, Amelia?" Septimus asked. Hesitating for a moment, she finally convinced herself that it would be alright. "What if there was a way that someone could preserve memories in a bottle? You know, like one would a scent or sand from the beach. And that way, whenever you were feeling down or just wanted to recall something pleasant, you could open the bottle and relive it all over again." Amelia expressed.

"Which ones would you put in your bottle?"

"This one."
Septimus chuckled slightly into his coffee mug. "Is the coffee really that good?"
Suddenly, Amelia felt herself become quite offended. She began to mentally kick herself for saying something so foolish, but at the same time; she could not believe that he would all of a sudden make fun of her in such a manner. "You don't have to treat me like I'm a child, you know. I know I am not like all of those other women you spend your time with, the ones who are far more mature and experienced; who have bobbed hair and wear black satin dresses." Amelia argued passionately. "But..."
"Well, you wouldn't be out with me if you were." Septimus countered, cutting her off before she can rant further.
"Then, why do you take me out day after day? If it is that you think I am so childish and ugly." Amelia felt suddenly frightened by the realization that this was all because he felt sorry for her somehow, and he was just taking her out as a way to make himself feel better about himself, for caring for someone so simple minded and lonely. How could she have been so stupid to think that anyone would want her for anything else? She asked herself. "You don't have to choose me to be your charity case. You shouldn't." Amelia got up from her seat and began to walk towards the exit of the cafe. She was not really sure how she would get back to the hotel, or how long it would take her. All she knew was that she could not bear to be in the presence of someone who had been so dishonest with her anymore. And, she deserved whatever hardship she would have to endure on the way back, as punishment for how much of a fool she had been in all of this. Allowing him to make her believe that there was any more to this than him simply being kind to her.
Amelia's storming away was abruptly interrupted by the grip of a strong hand on the back of her arm. Septimus had caught up to her and was now guiding her towards a small, border wall of the cafe, where he made her sit down. "Damn my kindness and my charity, because to be perfectly honest with you, I don't possess either of those. I never have. I only ask you out every day because I want you. I need you,

somehow. And don't ask me to try and explain why, because I couldn't tell you if I tried." Septimus calmed down for a moment once he sensed that Amelia was not just going to get up and storm off again. Letting out a deep exhale and running his long fingers through his head of thick, wavy, dark hair, he finally took a seat next to her on the wall. Leaning slightly towards her, just enough to cause his body to make contact with hers, he finally said after a long and thoughtful silence, "You are young enough to be my daughter you know, and I don't know what to do with you. All I know is that you have blotted out the past for me, blinding me to all of the harsh memories like the light of a thousand suns. It is the only way that I can explain how I feel." He paused for another moment and turned to look into her eyes. Amelia was not quite sure what to expect, and she felt as if she needed to brace herself for some sort of impact, but she was not sure what. "If you don't believe me, all you have to do is say so, and I will walk away right now." The words hit Amelia like a ton of bricks. She could not believe that he was really giving her as much power over him as he said.

"I have only stayed because of you, Amelia." Septimus says, sounding as if he was really pleading for her not to send him away.

"But I don't know any more about you than I did the first day we met." Amelia stated, unsure of what to tell him, as her mind and heart were now locked in a battle to the death as to what she should do next.

"Do you want me to go?" Septimus pleaded once more, not answering her statement.

Amelia found herself completely speechless and at a loss for what to do in this moment. There were too many thoughts scrambling around in her head at once, and all she knew was what she felt deep down in her heart. A warm tear suddenly trickled down her cold cheek, as she did all she felt that she could do in this moment and that was to shake her head.

"To hell with this!" Septimus reached in, clasping her small face with his strong warm hands, and pressed his full, soft lips to hers in a passionate kiss. A flood of tingling electricity rushed all over her as she began to see small, flashing lights behind her eye lids. She was now completely defenseless in the wake of his passion. And all she could do now was surrender and savor the touch and taste of him on her lips. Septimus pulled away, still holding her face in his hands, and looking deeply into her eyes as he gently wiped her tears away with his thumbs.

"Just promise me one thing," he said, finally.

"Anything," Amelia responded.

"You will never wear black satin." And, they both dwelled in the moment, smiling at one another as warmly as the sun that shone down upon them. Amelia felt now that it would be this moment that she would like to capture in a bottle and keep for all eternity, to relive over and over again whenever she wished.

****

Over the next several days, Amelia was reminded of how at one point or another all good things must come to an end. She was also reminded of the fact that she was being paid to be there with a grown woman, who needed someone to look after her as if she was some kind of child, even though she was perfectly capable of taking care of herself. She just chose not to. Amelia could only guess it was because she had an affinity for watching others suffer at the expense of her annoying existence, but for now it was keeping her fed and clothed, so she could not complain too much. Except for the fact that now it was getting in the way of her much needed time with Septimus. It had been almost a week since she had seen him and she could barely stand it. The yearning to be near him had reached the point of a physical ache that nearly made her sick. She would often find herself completely lost and consumed by the need to just catch a glimpse of him, when she was about the hotel with her employer. And that would quite literally drive her to utter distraction. There was no place in her mind for anything else but him. And, in her dreams at night, all she could feel was the touch of his lips on hers as well as other things that she dare not speak of to herself, much less anyone else.

When Mrs. Vandemere told her that she had organized a little party in her suite and had invited him, Amelia felt that she wanted to hit the old woman for dangling the false hope of getting to see him in front of her. Knowing that there was no way that being the man that he was, he would most certainly not attend such a function. Especially, if it was being sponsored by Mrs. Vandemere, who he could not stand to be in the company of for more than a few seconds at best. But she was then suddenly and pleasantly surprised to hear that indeed he had decided to attend the party. Amelia knew that deep down it was because he felt the same way as she. And, she could only imagine how much the separation had been driving him mad. She wondered just how much worse it had been for him than it had been for her. She was then bombarded with the images of him entering the suite without even being announced and rushing to her, taking her in his strong arms, and kissing her all over to the shock and awe of everyone else in the room. She knew however, that this was not the way things were done. Unless of course they were in some kind of a movie, and with the way that her life was currently going; this was definitely not the case. If so, the writer was not the most merciful of people. She found herself wishing for a way to track this person down and beg them to speed things up to the point where they would live happily ever after. If indeed that was what lay in store for them. If not, she prayed that the powers that be would somehow take pity on her, and end her misery now before she was utterly dashed upon the rocks of life once again.

Amelia was glad to see that against his better judgement, Septimus brought himself to attend the party. Even though, she could tell by his expression that he was suffering through every moment of it. His jaw staying a hard line, and he was obviously gritting his teeth so hard that she was surprised the entire room of people couldn't hear it.

However, Amelia did not have much time to concentrate on what was happening to him, as she was kept busy while the party was in full swing. She was running around, pretty much doubling as a glorified waitress and maid, making sure that everyone's drinks were topped up and the ashtrays were empty. She did not have time to do much more than catch small, knowing glances and listen to snatches of the one-sided conversation that the very drunk Mrs. Vandemere was having with Septimus. Unsurprisingly, she had him backed up against a wall far away from everyone else. Amelia watched sympathetically, as she could tell that he was drifting in and out of being present and doing his best to hold his own with the old woman.

"You know you really shouldn't spend the rest of your life hung up on a dead woman, even if you are still in a lot of pain. You see, it's not fair of you to deprive the rest of the female population this way. Such a waste, really, a strapping piece of man like you. I honestly don't think Persephone would want that for you." Mrs. Vandemere said.

"It is very kind of you to take it upon yourself to tell me such things, considering the fact that I barely know you, and Persephone never did. Excuse me," Septimus responded with gruff. He brushed past the frail, swaying Mrs. Vandemere, before making his way out of the crowded room of dancing strangers. All as drunk, if not more so than she.

Mrs. Vandemere rushed after him in a panic, grasping at the sleeve of his tuxedo in an effort to stop him from leaving. "Please, stay. Oh, don't leave like this. You just can't!" She stepped in front of him and placed her hands on his chest, bringing him to a temporary halt. Amelia watched in horror as Septimus seemed to grow in stature with his growing anger, towering over her employer.

"Everyone! I propose a toast! A toast to Persephone Creede!" Mrs. Vandemere raised her nearly empty glass far over her head, spilling some of her cocktail as she did. The music came to a halt, and everyone stopped and stared dumbfoundedly in the direction of Mrs. Vandemere and Septimus. Both standing smack in the center of the room. Everyone else unsure of whether to join in the toast or not. Everything else now still and quiet, like the calm before a great storm. Amelia felt that it was the loudest silence she had ever heard in all of her life, as she watched Septimus completely change colors from his customary pale complexion, to three different shades of an angry and fiery red. She feared that he would most certainly spontaneously combust at any moment, and the explosion would destroy all of them. But he only pushed his way past Mrs. Vandemere, his eyes nearly glowing red like the devil himself as he glared at everyone in the room. They all cowered and did their best to resume their previous distracting activities, doing what they could to disappear back into the party and forget the severity of the social blunder their host had just committed. Amelia raced after him, following him to the door where he stopped for a moment. He turned to face her. She racked her mind for something appropriate to say, but she felt that there were not any words strong enough to salve the gaping wound that Mrs. Vandemere had reopened for him. Nothing on heaven or earth would make for a worthy apology. The only thing that she found she could do was stand there and stare into his eyes in the most sorrowful way possible, wishing that there was something she could do. Begging him with her heart to please not blame her for any of this, and fearing that it would not be enough to keep him from leaving Provence all together. She felt a slight rage build up inside of herself as well at the thought that Mrs. Vandemere may have ruined her chances with him forever, and she was afraid that if this were to be the case, she would certainly not be responsible for any of her actions following this moment.

Septimus's expression softened only slightly as he looked into Amelia's eyes, telling her that she needn't fear losing him. Saving what was left of Mrs. Vandemere's life, Amelia observed to herself. She would live to fight another day, for now. There was still tomorrow.

He reached out and handed her the glass that remained in his hand, being sure to pass it to her with both hands so that his fingers grazed hers slowly. Her heart leapt within her as it had been several days since she had felt the touch of his skin on hers. It was all she could do to not jump forward and place a passionate kiss on his lips this very instant. But she listened to his wordless assurance that if she was patient, she would receive much more than a kiss. She just needed to be patient.

The next afternoon, Amelia found her way to the outdoor cafe that Septimus had taken her to all those days ago. Since there had been such an expanse of time between the last time she had seen him, all of those times together seemed like something out of a faraway dream. And, she was desperately doing everything she could to hold onto every sensation from those memories, for fear that somehow, she would forget them if she was not careful.

Upon entering the small, outdoor space, she was very glad to see that her hunch had been correct. Septimus and she had the same mind. He was here. As soon as he caught sight of her, he nearly bounded over to her, to take her in his arms. With his very long legs, his strides did not have to be many, and before she could blink, there he was. And then she was in his arms, with the warm touch of his lips placing kisses all over her face. Amelia smiled and giggled, feeling like a giddy fool. But she did not care, for she was with him, and she was not ashamed to say that he made her feel like such a giddy fool.

Finally returning her feet to the ground, Septimus guided her gently by the arm with his firm hand, over to a small stone water fountain that was now dry and overgrown with various wild greenery; where he invited her to sit down.

"I apologize for last night. I really made a mess of things, didn't I? You would think that at my age I would know better than to throw such a tantrum, like a little child. It was really very inexcusable of me." Septimus apologized in a quiet and reserved tone.

"Oh, no. There is really no need for you to take on so." Amelia placed her hand gently on his arm in a gesture of reassuring comfort. It was the only way she felt she could tell him that if anyone should be sorry, it was her for allowing it to happen in the first place. Though, she knew that if she voiced this, he would probably argue that she should not talk such nonsense, because she was not in any position to have done anything at all. So, she would just satisfy herself with this and do her best to not give him an excuse to talk to her like she was a child. Because recalling how well that worked out last time, she decided it was probably best to avoid anything that could remotely lead into any such conversation now. Or ever.

"Mrs. Vandemere can be a very unpredictable sort of woman at times. Well, all the time, really. It is because she is quite foolish and unhappy in her advancing age." Amelia tries to explain.

"To be pitied and patiently born, I suppose." Septimus commented with a bit of a sly smile that Amelia could not quite interpret, and she felt a bit frightened of the thoughts he may voice next. She was only grateful that there was no one else around to hear what he had to say. "I'm afraid that I am not the type that has ever been good at that sort of thing. Quite unfortunate really, isn't it? One of my many and probably worst defects, wouldn't you say? My dear." His eyes continued to glow, and his smile oozed with sarcasm. The arch of his eyebrow did not help much either in making Amelia feel at ease. She knew that she needed to be careful, for she was about to step into some sort of trap. He most certainly was far more experienced at playing this game of verbal repartee than she was.

"You're making fun of me again." Amelia said with a poignant eyebrow raise of her own.

"Oh, no...not really." Septimus tilted his head to the side to get a better look into her eyes, which were now looking down in the direction of her shoes. "It's just that you can be such an awfully solemn little thing at times."

"Oh, little thing? Is that how you see me?" Amelia raised her gaze to look into his eyes with a bit of indignance in her voice. Only to realize that the beaming smile on his face was because he had laid out the bait, and she was now officially caught. Why couldn't people like him just ask for you to look at them when they wanted you to pay attention? She asked herself as she shook her head and smiled back at him, blushing slightly in her embarrassment of losing this round.

"Don't be hurt by that, I didn't mean it to. I was just saying that I hope you will always be this way with me, natural and open." Septimus's voice became gentler with every word.

"What? Like a little girl who never grows up," she stated.

"No! I am not saying that at all!" Septimus looked at her, obviously caught by surprise. And then she victoriously watched a bit of a flush come to his face, as he realized that she may have just beaten him at his own game. Consider your goat truly gotten, sir, she wanted to say. But she was pleased enough to say this to herself. A bit of pride welling up within her chest.

Septimus's expression took on a more serious and philosophical tone, still keeping the softness that seemed to drape itself over his whole demeanor. "I am saying, Amelia, that I hope you will always be like you." He gathered her hand up into his and kissed it firmly.

"Well, it doesn't really matter how you see me. I will be gone in a few days and you will forget all about me." Amelia sighed heavily, only just now feeling the true weight of this realization herself.

"I am pretty certain I won't forget you." He reassured her, leaning his body into hers and resting his chin on her shoulder.

"What, your funny simple-minded little friend?" She asked, laying her head on his.

"No, you, of course. I could never forget you...as long as I lived. And, perhaps after."

Chapter 5

Amelia awoke the next day to find that the spring had once again returned to her step and she felt new. Like the morning after the first day that she had met Septimus. All seemed to be right with the world. There were several instances during her morning routine, where she heard the sound of a woman humming, as she was bathing and getting dressed for the day. Only to stop and realize that the voice she heard singing and humming so happily was her own. She was so perfectly and incandescently happy, that she believed that there was truly nothing in the world that could ruin this feeling for her, not even if it tried.

Until suddenly, when she burst into Mrs. Vandemere's portion of the suite. She was greeted by the horrifying sight of various open suitcases and trunks everywhere. The fear settled on her like an overwhelming weight, and her head began to spin. She felt her stomach dropping without warning and her heart rising into her throat, creating a pulsing sensation that resounded through the whole of her head and threatened to make her skull explode. She was sure that at any moment her brain would implode, and she waited for the feeling of its warm fluids to suddenly come rushing out of her ears and down her neck. But the sensation never came. How merciless life could be sometimes. She only hoped that everything Septimus had said only a day before was true. Because, that would be the only thing that the two of them would be able to hang onto. It would all be but a memory, once Mrs. Vandemere whisked her away from here to god knows where. If she was lucky, she would have a hankering to go to the English country side. But unfortunately, it was not exotic enough of a destination for Mrs. Vandemere. So, all that was left for Amelia to do was stand there and suffer in suspense, as she waited for Mrs. Vandemere to get off the phone and tell her what far away, other side of the universe, destination she had in mind.

"It would serve you very well to remember who I am. If I need to, I have no problem with coming down there and straightening out all of your asses in person. No sir! If this is not taken care of by the time I am ready to check out in the morning, you will be hearing from my attorney." Mrs. Vandemere punctuated her statement by slamming the receiver of the phone back onto the bell box. A loud ringing trailed off into the intense silence of the room that lay between her and Amelia, as Amelia was too afraid to even draw breath now. Or was it that her mind was too full to even remember how to fill her lungs anymore? She couldn't be sure.

Mrs. Vandemere hopped off the top of the writing desk on which she sat, with a happy skip and a sway of her bony, fragile hips. Amelia found herself hoping very much that somehow, just then, she would slip and break one of them.

Thus, buying them some more time. And to her further surprise, she discovered that she was not in the least bit apologetic for fostering this particular train of thought. Love really does drive people mad, doesn't it? She questioned herself.

"Guess what, my pet? We are packing up this carnival and leaving for New York!" Mrs. Vandemere declared happily.

"What is that look for? You look as if I told you someone just ran over your dog." She nudged Amelia's dropped chin with a crooked and wrinkled finger. Amelia remained silent. There were too many things running around in her mind just now, for her to even begin to attempt forming any kind of a relatively intelligible sentence.

"You really should be grateful, you know." Mrs. Vandemere began again, but then paused for a moment to look into her eyes, trying to decipher what was going on in Amelia's mind. "What happened, honey? I thought you didn't like Europe. You know, the two of you don't really have good history and all that."

"Well, I suppose I got used to it. It's sort of grown on me, I guess." Amelia finally said, doing her best to prevaricate about the true reason why she desperately did not want to leave.

"Then, I suppose you can just get used to New York. Trust me hun, it won't take long for it to grow on you either."

"When do we leave?" Amelia asked, hoping that somehow the answer would change from what she had just told the front desk over the phone. But she knew that it was probably worthless to hope any further.

"We blow this popsicle stand in the morning, so you best get packing. The sooner the better, sweet cheeks."

Later that night, Amelia was racked with violent waves of grief like she had never experienced before. Not even when they informed her that Gregory was declared missing in action. This was something completely different. She knew now why they said that *'hope deferred maketh the heart sick.'* For both she and her heart were now truly sick, sick with overwhelming grief. Amelia now completely understood all of those love stories where the woman would throw herself from a widow's walk for the love of a man. They usually hit hard. All those stories that she had previously found to be so silly, she could now suddenly picture herself doing just the same thing. If she could not have Septimus, then she wanted nothing at all. Especially not the prospect of living an entire life time without him, and being made to wonder what might have been, if she had just somehow found a way to stay here with him.

Amelia stopped crying for a moment and pulled her head out of her pillow, which was now soaking wet from absorbing all of her tears, and muffling the sounds of her loud, hiccupping, unladylike sobs. The thought hit her like a strong gust of wind, and all of the emotional cobwebs in her mind were blown away, revealing the realization that she only had one option now. She needed to see him. Even if it may be for the last time. She had the feeling that just by making the move to go see him, even now, while it was still in the middle of the night; he would be able to come up with some way that would prevent this terrible tragedy from befalling her. Befalling the both of them.

Amelia quickly jumped out of bed and threw on her dressing gown. She quietly and swiftly snuck out of her room and through the main room of the suite, making sure on her way that Mrs. Vandemere was still soundly sleeping. She also stopped for a moment to debate just how difficult it would be to smother her with a pillow. But she quickly brushed the thought away, and told herself that the longer she stood there thinking such nonsensical thoughts, the more she was wasting valuable time. Time that she could be using to come up with a better solution to her problem, a solution that did not end in her going to the gallows. However, if that was the price that she had to pay for his love, in this moment, it did not seem that steep. And she would gladly pay it if it were to come to that. She made her way down the maze of hallways throughout the hotel, in search of his room. Only realizing as she made it to his door, that in her haste, she had forgotten to put on her house slippers. But that did not matter much to her right now. A slight chill traveled up and down her slender legs in the drafty hallway, as she hesitated with her fist only inches away from his door. It was still the middle of the night, and she could only imagine how foolish he would think her for calling on him at such an hour, for something that they would probably have plenty of time to speak of in the morning before she left. Amelia second guessed herself for a moment, as she could almost hear him saying these things to her.

Once again, her heart overrode her mind, propelling her fist forward and making her knock on the solid oak door. She made sure not to do it loud enough to disturb the rest of the patrons in the neighboring rooms. The last thing either of them needed right now, was for a spectacle to be made of the fact that a young woman was coming to his room in the middle of the night. What a scandal that would be?

It seemed like an eternity, despite the fact that Amelia was sure it was only a few seconds ago she heard someone on the other side of the door, and saw a slice of light pour out from under it as someone turned on the lamp in the small entry way. Suddenly, the door swung open, causing her to jump with a start, and let out a slight, squeaky gasp. She placed her hands over her mouth quickly to muffle the sound.

Septimus stood there in the doorway of the suite. The dim light of the solitary lamp in the entryway behind him, caused his tall and ominous figure to appear like a frightening silhouette in the back lighting. There he stood, his hair disheveled, with the traces of his face only shown in the fire light of the cherry from his cigarette, smoke coming from his nostrils and lips like some kind of a dragon. Seeing him like this shocked Amelia almost as much as his abrupt opening of the door. She had never seen him in such an unkempt manner before. She could tell that he had not been sleeping either, and she wondered if this was because he did not usually sleep, or if it was because he somehow knew what was happening before she had even told him. Amelia continued to hesitate, knowing that his reaction to what she said next would tell her whether his feelings for her were genuine or not. But she needed to know.

"Mrs. Vandemere is leaving for New York in the morning, and I just wanted to say good-bye, for I didn't know whether I would have the chance to tel..." Amelia began explaining in a shaky and timid voice.

"No," Septimus interrupted in a stern voice, grabbing her roughly by the arm and pulling her into the room. Then, closing the door with a loud slam behind her.

Amelia sat there quietly on the small sofa in the parlor of his suite, watching as he paced back and forth deep in thought, surrounded by a heavy cloud of tobacco smoke as he continued to chain smoke. Even though he was the perfect portrait of a man on the threshold of madness, with his sprawling and spiked black hair, patchy and shiny skin, and a jaw lined with a little bit more than traces of a five o'clock shadow, she somehow found that she was more attracted to him looking this way, than she ever had been when he was clean and more polished. He seemed to be more human, more vulnerable this way. And she felt as if she were privileged somehow for him to allow her to see him this way.

"So, Mrs. Vandemere has grown tired of Europe and has decided to move her hunting ground to New York, hmm? And inevitably you are obligated to go with her." Septimus pulled another cigarette from the box on the table and tapped the end against the tabletop to pack in the loose tobacco.

"Yes, unfortunately." Amelia said in a sad whisper.

  Suddenly, he looked up from the surface of the table, throwing a lingering and thoughtful side glance in Amelia's direction. She felt as if she could almost hear the wheels turning his head, as he began to craft some sort of plan. Amelia knew then that she had come to the right place, but at the same time she found herself quite afraid of what he was about to suggest next.

"But, what if you didn't." Septimus said more as a statement rather than a question.

"You mean as some kind of secretary or something?" Amelia asked, afraid of what he was actually suggesting, yet hoping that he was saying exactly what she believed he was trying to imply.

"No, I am asking you to marry me, you fool!" Septimus clarified gruffly, shaking his head as though he couldn't believe she would think that he was offering her a job. Amelia shrank back into the sofa, shocked by not only the declaration of his intentions, but by the manner in which he made them known to her. Septimus let out a heavy exhale and took a seat next to her, gathering her hands into his in a gesture of gentleness and caring.

"I apologize." He looked into her eyes. "I realize that this is awfully sudden and most certainly not the best way to propose, I'm sure. The scenario should play out more traditionally. You in a beautiful dress and the setting more romantic. I know you probably pictured something like a garden or conservatory, you standing there with a rose in your hand. But time is of the essence here, if we are going to stay together."

Amelia nodded, knowing that everything he said was true. And despite the great feelings of what she could only think of as love that she had developed for him, there was still something incomplete within her that she could not quite explain. From the time that she met him only a couple of weeks prior until now, everything had been moving almost in fast forward. Now that he had voiced the truth that everything was taking place so suddenly, she began to wonder if it all was happening too rapidly. Was she rushing into this because of the desperation to sate her loneliness? And did she completely love him? or was this just some flight of fancy that would peter out after a time, with the drudgery of everyday life?

Septimus seemed crushed by the silence of her hesitation and look of confusion. Amelia began to wonder if he was able to hear her argue with herself, as his face turned very solemn when he removed his hands from hers and looked down at his bare feet. "I don't know what I was thinking, of course this is too sudden." He threw his hands up slightly. "But I thought you loved me."

Amelia scooted in closer to him and placed her hand on his arm, "Oh, but I do love you." She felt slightly unsure about how completely genuine her statement was, but she assured herself that with time, she was sure that she would be able to love him as much as he deserved. All they needed was time and if she did not take him up on his offer now, they would never have any time ever again.

"Does that mean, yes?" Septimus turned to her, hope in his eyes.

"Yes," Amelia nodded and smiled.

Clasping his hands around her face, he pulled her in for a kiss. The touch of his lips wiping away any inhibitions, fears, or reservations she had about going away with him. Pulling away slightly, Septimus looked deeply into her eyes, his own eyes gleaming with an incredible and heavenly happiness. Amelia felt almost magical as she saw a bright light begin to pour in around them and start to illuminate the rest of the room around them. Then, glancing over to the two great windows behind them, she realized that the sun had started to come up, and was now dappling its young rays through the sheer curtains that covered them.

"I suppose someone had better tell Mrs. Vandemere." Amelia commented with a sly grin.

"I nearly forgot all about her. I can do that for you, if it will make it easier." Septimus offered, brushing her long flaxen hair out of her face.

"No, that's alright. I think I can handle it. Besides, I think it would probably be best if the news came from me." Amelia leaned her face into the warm caress of his palm and placed a fervent kiss upon it.

"I suppose you're right."

****

Amelia made her way back through the maze of halls and all the way back to Mrs. Vandemere's suite, with a skip in her step and a song in her heart. She did not care that she was walking through the now populated corridors of people who were already dressed to the nines, in readiness for the rest of their day. Her own self sticking out in her dressing gown and night dress like a vagrant at a wedding, her feet still completely bare. She greeted every strange look with a smile and a nod of her head, telling each and every one of them just how much she did not care what they thought of her strange appearance. Amelia could only imagine the kind of thoughts and speculations running through all of their small and prudish minds. But it did not bother her, for this was certainly no walk of shame for her, and she did not feel that they deserved any sort of explanation on her part. For she was about to be Mrs. Septimus Creede, and from that point on she would no longer have to furnish anyone with an explanation or argument for anything she decided to do ever again.

Finally, she reached the door of Mrs. Vandemere's suite, where she burst in with a confident flare and closed the door suddenly behind her. There she stood in front of the door, staring at Mrs. Vandemere as she walked about the room that now resembled more of an obstacle course, as it was still littered with all of the old woman's trunks and suit cases, all in various stages of emptiness and fullness. She waited for her to turn around and notice that she had even come into the room.

Mrs. Vandemere turned around, clasping the pearls that hung in a long chain around her sagging and wrinkled neck, as if she were startled by the sudden appearance of Amelia. "Oh, child! You really must announce yourself when you come into a room. I am not as young as I appear, you know, and the last thing you need is for me to have a heart attack." Mrs. Vandemere scolded in a somewhat breathless tone as she tried to regain her composure. "Good thing you're here now, I never know where you are nowadays. You are never here when I need you...and what are you wearing?" Mrs. Vandemere waved her pince-nez up and down in a manner to frame Amelia's appearance in the air in front of her, like the wave of a wand by a fairy godmother. Amelia remained silent, basking in the glow of the bomb that she was about to drop on the old woman. If she thought that she nearly gave her a heart attack by walking into the room, she wondered for a moment if by telling her the news, that might actually finish her off. This caused her to once again begin to debate with herself whether she should say anything or just make her way to her room quietly, gather the rest of her things, and just leave without a single indication that she was going to disappear at all. Flitting away like the ghost that Mrs. Vandemere always accused her of looking like.

"Well, my dear, the sooner we get finished with the packing the sooner we can get out of here. I don't think I can stand to be here another minute. New York here we come!" Mrs. Vandemere said, while closing the lid on one of her smaller caboodles.

"Well, I am afraid that you will have to make the journey without me, Mrs. Vandemere." Amelia states finally after her long silence.

"Oh, and why is that?" Mrs. Vandemere asked in quiet surprise, but with a slight, sly glimmer in her eyes.

"You will have to go without me because I am leaving your employ." Amelia responded very dryly and matter-of-factly.

"Why? Is there something I have done to make you feel this way?" Mrs. Vandemere interrogated.

"It is not so much a matter of anything that you have done, ma'am. You have been very good to me. It is just that I am getting married." Amelia explained.

Mrs. Vandemere was so taken aback by this statement that she nearly fell to the floor, only saving herself by catching her hands on the desk behind her and slowly sitting up against it.

"Wha...um...why...who?" Mrs. Vandemere finally squeezed out the words with great difficulty. Looking around herself as if somehow, she would find the answer on the floor.

"Septimus Creede," Amelia said just as plainly and without emotion as she had declared everything else just now.

"Ah ha, I see!" Mrs. Vandemere slapped her own thigh and began to wag her finger in Amelia's direction. Her face, voice, and demeanor taking on the air of just how flabbergasted she was by the suddenness of the news. "I know what you were doing now, my girl, tennis lessons indeed! Huh!"

"You don't have to worry, Mrs. Vandemere, I was not planning on leaving you in the lurch, completely. I will finish packing the big trunk for you before I go." Amelia informed her kindly.

"Oh, don't worry Mrs. Vandemere I'm not leaving you in the lurch..." Mrs. Vandemere repeated in a voice mocking

Amelia's. "Don't even bother! I should have known that something like this would happen, that you would betray me like this."

"Betray you? I haven't done..."

"Oh, but haven't you?! You see, I have always known that it is the quiet ones that you have to watch out for. Don't let my looks fool you, my mind is not one of a spring chicken. I...I wasn't born yesterday." She was now pacing about the room as she ranted in her displeasure.

Amelia restrained herself against the temptation of telling Mrs. Vandemere that it was quite clear she had not been born yesterday, or possibly even in this century.

Mrs. Vandemere calmed herself momentarily and took a more thoughtful and strategic pose against the desk once again, chewing the end of her pince-nez, and her thin, red penciled, eyebrow arched far enough to almost touch her faintly receding hairline. "Just tell me this, little girl, are you prepared for what you have let yourself in for? Hmm? Are you ready for the tiger that you have let into your bed? Septimus is an awful lot of man to please, and you...still practically a virgin, are certainly not properly equipped to please someone like him. Are you sure you're ready for that, missy?"

Amelia felt the indignation rise within her, and she wanted nothing more than to rush over and slap the smug look from Mrs. Vandemere's cragged face. But instead she decided to storm away into her assigned quarters and gather the rest of her things. She no longer had time to stand there and deal with her employer's pettiness, and she didn't have to. Mrs. Vandemere was no longer her employer. She was completely free. Free to start this new and exciting chapter in her life as the lady of Creede Castle, and that is all that needed to matter to her now.

Amelia flung herself onto the bed in a supine position and gazed up at the decorative ceiling of her suite room one last time, letting out a heavy and pleasant sigh of relief. The magical, tingling sensation she had experienced just this morning began washing over her body once again, as she recalled the memory of his soft lips on hers, and the rough yet soft caress of his hands on her face. A great smile crept its way onto her face as she closed her eyes in a dreamy state, feeling as if she would surely melt into some kind of cloud and fly away. She quietly whispered to herself, now finally experiencing the reality and weight of the words that made her feel as light as a feather. "Mrs. Septimus Creede."

Chapter 6

Just as rapidly as everything had happened before, it seemed to accelerate even more once she and Septimus began their journey back towards England. They married in Paris, and continued to make their way through the rest of Europe as a sort of impromptu honeymoon. Septimus told her that this was his way of making it up to her for the hasty way that he had proposed, and it was more than enough to help her forgive him. Even though, she felt that there was not really anything to forgive. They finally made their way onto a ship that was bound for England. It was a beautiful cruise liner, like nothing she had ever seen before. Not just any kind of passenger ship that was simply meant to take people to and fro, across the channel. It was fully equipped with everything one could possibly imagine that they needed, as well as a few things that they probably did not, but that did not matter. This only added to the grand spectacle that was this bright city that sailed over the water.

However, Amelia did not find that she had much time to experience much of the things that ship itself had to offer, as she was too busy doing other more important things. And, to what she would imagine would be Mrs. Vandemere's great chagrin and jealousy, she found out that she was fully equipped to please Septimus, over and over again.

Amelia observed to herself that she had never spent quite so much time in bed in her life. Not even when she was going through her depression. Needless to say, this was far more of a pleasant experience than that would ever be. She was spending her days of late just lying there, her petite and delicate frame tightly held to his vastly contrasting tall and mighty form. Experiencing every rise and fall of his powerful breath, and the sound of his rapturous beating heart. Even just thinking about feeling the weight of his body on top of hers, comfortably crushing her, was enough to make her swoon and feel as if she were going to melt into a compliant puddle at any moment. He was her addiction now; she could not be without him. And she believed whole heartedly that he felt the same way about her, and he was certainly not bashful about showing it in the secluded den they had made out of their ship's cabin.

Amelia lay there, her head resting on his slowly undulating chest, basking in the afterglow. Closing her eyes, she allowed herself to take in the sensation of feeling the soft and supple skin of his pectorals and stomach, under her delicate finger tips. She closed her eyes even tighter as she felt his fingers make their way up the back of her neck, causing a rush of goosebumps to cover the rest of her body. His strong hand was in her hair now, at the back of her head, where he massaged lightly, before suddenly taking a handful of her hair in his hand and pulling her head back gently so she was forced to face him. Septimus looked deeply into her eyes with dark and beautiful mysterious pools of the deepest black you had ever seen, peering into her bright, crystalline, green eyes. They were truly so opposite, but in moments like this they melded so well together. Amelia's breath caught short as she anticipated his next move, which was to lean in and place a tender but passionate kiss on her now waiting, full and hungry lips. The strength of his masterful tongue pressing its way into her mouth and rubbing hers. Never had she known love like this, and she wondered often at times like this if she were living or if she had been transported to some fantasy-like eternity. She surely must be in heaven.

Pulling away, and leaving her now warm and wanting, he said, "At some point, I suppose, we are going to have to leave this cabin. Even if it is only for our last night here on the ship." He continued to comb his fingers through her hair.

"Oh, but why? Do we have to?" Amelia whined, as she poked out her bottom lip in a gesture of pleading sadness and disappointment, knowing that he was probably right. But she did not want this to end.

Septimus leaned in and lightly grazed her puckered lip with his teeth, causing her to giggle quietly. "If we don't, people might get the idea we are some kind of animals that just can't stand to keep our hands off of each other."

"And, that would be a bad thing?" Amelia asked with a naughty glint in her eye.

"Naughty," he playfully scolded her as he touched the end of her nose with his index finger. Septimus grunted reluctantly as he rolled over and climbed out of the bed. Leaving Amelia to lay where he once was. She whimpered as he walked away, pulling his hand from hers, as she tried to keep him in the bed with her.

Amelia watched him from behind as he walked away towards the bathroom of the cabin. Laying there, her eyes scanned his wonderful, naked form up and down. He was really quite a magnificent example of manliness for someone who claimed to be so much older than she. His body certainly showed no overt signs of being over forty.

Continuing to bask in the warmth of her feelings, her mind began to wander once again into thoughts of just how quickly things had changed for her. In just a short amount of time, she had transformed completely from a quiet, little mouse of a person, content to be completely invisible, to someone who was now loved by someone as wonderful as he. How was it that she had found herself to be deserving of such happiness? How in the world did she ever get to be so lucky?

After reluctantly getting dressed, Amelia felt very strange to be wearing clothes now, after having spent so much of her time lately not wearing anything at all. She also felt a deep emptiness within herself, as she was now wandering about the ship without Septimus. It was as if they had been joined at the hip since they had set off across Europe. And, especially, after they had boarded the ship. But she had to remember that Septimus was still a formidable captain of industry with a life outside of her. And right now, he needed to make some calls to London, as well as call home and make sure that everything was amply prepared for their arrival. Even though he made her feel as if she was the only thing that existed on the planet whenever they were together, she needed to remember that the world as far as he was concerned, did not completely revolve around her.

He had spoiled her really, and as much as she loved this about him. She knew that now that she was his wife, she was going to have to take the fact that he had other obligations in stride, and endure the fact that he could not be with her every second of the day. Amelia scolded herself, as well as laughed to herself, at how she was now in such a silly frame of mind. Never had she ever thought that she would feel this way ever again, about anyone. A glimmer of regret tugged at her heart as she realized that she had all but forgotten about Gregory. And, she wondered for a moment if she should be ashamed of herself, or if this is what her once beloved Gregory would have wanted for her. Would he be alright with the fact that she was not spending her days thinking about him? Was she killing him all over again, by filling her mind with thoughts of love for someone else?

She stopped her meandering walk and thoughts for a moment, as she looked at her own reflection in the window of one of the many shops that lined the inside of the ship. Gazing deeply into her own eyes, she saw that they were now fuller and brighter. The color had returned to her face that had once lived there when she was a bit younger. She finally appeared to be happy. Gregory always told her she looked her most beautiful when she was happy. She always figured that it was his way of consoling her when she would feel inadequate, for not being able to afford things like lipstick or rouge when she wanted to look beautiful for him. He told her that her happiness was enough for him, and she needn't worry about comparing herself to anyone else because she would always be enough, as long as she was happy. This was all the comfort that she needed just now. Amelia lingered there for another moment, fancying that she could almost hear his voice whispering in her ear, telling her that she did not have to worry about him anymore. The only thing he ever cared about in the world was her happiness.

Amelia drew a deep and slightly ragged, tear-filled breath, as she retrieved a handkerchief from her pocket and began to wipe the mistiness from her face.

"Oh, dear, pat, don't rub." Amelia heard the voice of an older woman reach out to her and suddenly grasp her ear. Amelia looked around in a start, unsure of where the voice had originated. Looking over to one side, she realized that there was a well-dressed elderly woman standing in the doorway of the shop where she had been standing, for what she felt was entirely too long now. "If you rub, it makes your face look all red and patchy. Nobody wants to be seen like that. Especially, a pretty little girl like yourself, my dear."

Amelia smiled and looked down shyly. "I suppose you're right." She chuckled quietly, putting the handkerchief back into her pocket.

"I know I am, dear. Did you see something you liked?" The lady asked, waving her hand invitingly into the shop.

"Oh, no. I'm sorry I was just..." Amelia began to decline her offer, when suddenly something in the window caught her eye. In her observation of her own reflection, she had not noticed it before, and now it seemed to be calling to her from within. There she stood for a moment, seeing the reflection of her face positioned perfectly at the top of the neck of the headless mannequin in the window, making it appear as if she were wearing the dress herself. "You know, I think I do." Amelia smiled at the woman, whose grin became bigger as she took the timid Amelia by the hand and guided her into the shop.

It did not take very long for the woman to get the dress off from the form of the lithe, stark white, figure that stood stationary on the pedestal, beckoning on people to purchase what it was offering. A long, black, silk number covered in sparkling little black stones. It was definitely far more daring than the plain beige or mousy brown cotton fabrics that she was accustomed to wearing. There were no sleeves to be spoken of, and the neckline draped far down, accentuating every curve of her womanly form. Showing that she indeed possessed breasts that hung firmly and deliciously, like ripe fruit ready to be devoured.

Stepping out of the fitting room and looking at herself in the tall mirror, she felt a slight twinge of apprehension, as this was truly more daring than she had ever endeavored to look in her life. Who was this...woman, who stood before her now? This creature that glared at her with a fierce, empowered fire, that was completely unknown and foreign to her. Surely, it was not she. It couldn't be. Or could it?

"Oh, my." The clerk gasped. "You are utterly stunning, my dear." The woman observed as she came in behind Amelia and began to stroke back her long locks of golden hair like a loving grandmother would, as she looked upon the finally grown up form of her beloved granddaughter.

"I don't know, if this is really my style, though. It's so powerful. So..." Amelia searched for the right words.

"Grown up," the clerk added, and Amelia knew that this was the precise term. "You look like a real woman."

"You're right, I do." Amelia placed her hands on her hips and turned from side to side to inspect her appearance further, lifting the skirt of the dress slightly to take a look at how well defined and womanly her legs appeared, now that she was wearing shoes with a heel. Nothing too extreme, but still, it was not anything she would ever think of herself wearing before. And, even though she wanted desperately to like it, she found herself almost afraid to. It would be one more change, the true closing of the last chapter of her life, and she wasn't sure if she was ready to completely put her other self to death just yet. Even with as small of a gesture as changing her appearance.

"Except of course, for this lovely long hair. You know no one over eighteen wears their hair this long these days, not anymore." The clerk commented.

"No they don't, do they?" Amelia observed out loud, more to herself than in reply to what the clerk had said.

"I am not saying that you have to cut it, dear, for it is lovely.
But it makes you look so…"
"Childish." Amelia added, realizing it to herself as well.
"I was going to say young, but…yes. If I may be so bold to
say."
"You may,"
"We have a salon here, where we can take care of that, too;
for just a little extra, of course."
"Of course, that is no trouble." Amelia couldn't believe those
words were actually passing from her lips with any form of
seriousness. She had never been in a place financially where
she could treat money as if it was no object.
"Shall we? It's right this way," The clerk gestured, and Amelia
followed, with no further apprehensions about not only
changing her appearance, but what she surely felt would be
taking the next step into the rest of her grown life.

After only a couple of hours of primping and fussing, she was
ready. Amelia's new look was complete. Her hair bobbed and
slightly highlighted, and she had even decided to take things
a step further and allow the woman to match her with a
foundation, mascara, and lipstick. The boldest shade of
oxblood red that she could find. She looked and felt like a
completely different woman. Woman. The word that had
intimidated her for so long before, now filled her with pride
and power. Things were going well for her finally, and she
was grateful. She could now look at the other members of
society around her that were long time card holding
members of this order of ultimate female, and not cower in
her inadequacies in their presence. For she was now one of
them, a grown woman, and she looked the part. 'It took me
long enough', she thought to herself in a slightly scolding
manner. The only thing that mattered was the fact that she
had taken the measures to make it happen, not how long it
took her to get there. And, she was sure that Septimus would
probably tell her the same thing if she were to ask him. She
was finally worthy to stand up next to him. They would be
the complete and perfect picture of two people who were

prepared to take on life. Making wealth and power look like it was an easy burden to bear.

Amelia walked with confidence in her stride as she made her way to the ship's restaurant, where Septimus told her to meet him after he had concluded all of his business. 'Such a gentlemen he was, in every sense of the word', she thought. Doing everything he could to make her life seem as easy as possible, and not to worry her with all of the logistics that were required to keep their life such as it was. And, she was now resolved to do her dead level best, to play the part of the perfect and respectable wife who would soothe him. Being the warm and welcoming arms for him to fall in, after a long day of carrying the weight of their world. Her heroic atlas. He really was like a god to her in a way. A guardian angel, and she would be eternally grateful to him for rescuing her from not only the harshness of her previous life, but from herself. Upon arriving at the restaurant, she noticed that the wait staff immediately treated her differently than they had before, when she was dressed as she had been previously. They were now more accommodating and servant like, as if she was some sort of royalty, warranting only the best treatment that they could possibly give her. Amelia smiled graciously at the obviously intimidated young man, who could not have been much older than her, as he asked if there was anything that he could do for her. Calling her milady. This was something that she was going to have to get accustomed to. She informed him that she was meeting her husband, Mr. Septimus Creede, yet another thing that she was going to have to get used to. He made very quick work of pointing him out to her, and offered to escort her down the small flight of steps and to the table. To this she declined politely, but she tipped him for his consideration anyway, to which he was more than grateful and made sure to tell her so.

Amelia decided to take the long way around when walking to the table, as a way to get the element of surprise when revealing her new and improved look, to what she was sure would be a more than pleased Septimus. Walking up behind him, she waited for a moment before making her presence known to him as he sat alone at the table, sipping his whiskey neat.

"Is this seat taken, Mr. Creede?" Amelia asked in the most seductive voice she can muster.

Septimus stood and turned around with a start, only to sit back down again suddenly in his shocked state.

"I was sure this would get a reaction, but I didn't think it was that shocking." Amelia said.

Septimus sat there for a long while, glaring at her in silence, as though he were unsure of what to say. Or trying to control himself to keep from shouting at her. She was not sure why she got this impression. But she waited silently for him to speak first.

"My god, Amelia! What have you done to yourself? What is that muck all over your face?" Septimus inquired, obviously in a great state of displeasure. This caused Amelia to once again feel the sensation of self-doubt and inadequacy creep back into her spirit. She began to scramble for something to say that would somehow appease him before he made too much of a scene.

"Is it too much? It was really more sort of a joke, really? I'm sorry. I saw the other women..." She started trying to find anything that would sate his anger and defuse the situation before it completely imploded. "I thought it would go better with the dress."

Why was he not more pleased? She wondered to herself.

"Well, I didn't exactly marry a whore now, did I? At least, I didn't think I did." Septimus declared, as he hurriedly pulled the handkerchief from his lapel pocket.

"Septimus! Please," Amelia blurted out, shocked that he would use such language to refer to her.

"Wipe it off! Now!" He barked gruffly, grabbing at her wrist to force the slip of fabric into her hand.

"No, not here. I won't, I can't."

"You will do as I tell you, damnit! Wipe it off, now!" He stood up and gripped her forcibly, shoving the kerchief into her palm. Causing everyone sitting at the neighboring tables to stop their idle chatter and stare at them in shock.

The room began to spin around Amelia as she became sick and enraged. Her face now flushed and hot with humiliation and deep mortification. How could he have made such a fool out of her in front of all of these people? Who was this man and what had he done with the gentleman that she knew him to be?

"Why are you just standing there like an idiot? Take it off now!" Septimus shouted at her once again.

Amelia could not stand there any longer. All of the eyes on her, pitying her and jeering at her as she was being reprimanded like some kind of naughty child. All of the anxiety she had felt before, when she would walk the streets of her home town all came flooding back. She could not stand to be pitied and cajoled, even just by people's glances and silent thoughts. That was certainly worse than listening to what they were actually thinking. She turned and ran as quickly as her petite legs could carry her, out of the restaurant and back to the cabin. She could only imagine what all of those people thought of them, of her. They probably were speculating about how he most likely beats her when no one is looking. And she began to wonder as she locked herself in the small bathroom of the cabin, if that was what she was in for next. She knew that she had rushed into this. If only she had listened to the voice of her conscience before making this rash, and now very clearly unwise decision.

Tears welled up in her eyes, blurring her vision. The only thing that she could make out were the droplets of black ink from her eyeliner and mascara, which cascaded down her now red-hot face, and fell like a driving rain onto her hands, ultimately pooling in her small palms. What a cruel trick life had played on her this time. Betrayal washed over her like the warm, salt water of her tears that continued to fall with no sign of stopping. Her heart fell heavy in her chest and into the pit of her stomach that was now sick. She feared that if she continued like this, she would certainly vomit before too long. But there was no way that she could curb this sensation. She was well and truly lost for what to do next. Just when she thought that everything was finally looking up for her, the curtain had been pulled back to reveal nothing but more and worse trials awaiting her on the other side. The grass was certainly not greener on the other side of this fence. It was all brown, prickly, scorched and covered in sticker bushes and thorns. What had she done to deserve this? What was it they used to tell her at the group home, the toughest trials are reserved for the strongest warriors? Well, Amelia had news for the powers that be in the universe, there must have been a mix up between her and another Amelia; because she was certainly not as strong as they believed her to be. Not one bit. This was it; she was ready to give up. Especially, if it meant that things were just going to continue this way.

Suddenly, there was a soft but firm knock on the door that she sat up against, sending vibrations through the small of her back and causing her to sit up. Slightly fearful, she looked up to confirm to herself that she had taken the precaution to lock the door. This reassurance of her own forethought, allowed her to breathe a slow and ragged sigh of relief that she had not lost all sense of her faculties. With how clearly stupid she had been to accept his sudden proposal of marriage, and letting herself in for this sort of treatment, she began to wonder about herself. Just how much sense did she really have? Maybe she was an idiot as he said that she was.

"Amelia?" Septimus called out from the other side of the door. She remained silent.

"I am so sorry. I really shouldn't have treated you in such a manner. That was very beastly of me, wasn't it?" Amelia listened as he continued to speak, being careful not to move or make even the slightest of sounds. "Really? How could I have been so stupid? I feel like such a fool to get angry over a smear of lipstick, and a new haircut." He sighed loudly. "I know all you were trying to do was amuse me and I went and bit your head off. It was just the fact that you had changed yourself so much that scared me. You just took me by surprise, my darling. I promise I will never be so horrible to you ever again." He sighed again and his voice became more desperate. "Please say that you will forgive me...I...I couldn't live with myself if you won't forgive me."

Taking a deep, cleansing breath, Amelia gathered herself
from the tile floor and stood to her feet. Not bothering to
check her appearance in the mirror, which she could only
imagine to be probably a ghastly thing to behold. She slowly
opened the door to find him on his knees, on the floor in
front of her, on the other side of the door. Amelia knelt down
onto her knees and lifted up his solemn and sad face in her
hands. "Of course, I will forgive you." She watched as his eyes
brightened suddenly and relief washed over his face. Amelia
kissed him tenderly before he took her in his arms and
embraced her tightly.
As she lay her head on his shoulder, the thoughts began to
run their course through her mind once again. Telling her
that this may not have been the best situation to get herself
into, considering this man was going to throw such a tantrum
over the fact that she no longer looks like a child. But despite
this, she needed to remind herself that sometimes you don't
make the right decision. Sometimes there is nothing left to
do but make the decision right, and live with it as best you
can. She had made her bed and now she was going to have to
lie in it, no matter what that would entail for her in the
future. Good or bad, it was well and truly her burden to bear
now.

Chapter 7

The next morning came very quickly, and though everything seemed brighter with the sun and chatter of happy people around them, all eager to make their way home, Amelia still felt the weight of what she knew was now her new responsibility. She was going to have to live with the decision that she had made so rashly; to rush off with this man that she had barely known. And now, she was going to have to pay the hefty price that was required of her by the consequences. If she had learned anything by now, it was that life was certainly not like a fairy tale. A fact that from the events of last night, she was being well and truly educated in, and the quicker she caught on to this, the better it would be for her. She had painted herself into a corner, and now she was going to have make the best of it until such a time as the paint had dried, and she could walk out of there. Only God knew when that was going to be, so she decided to return to her more reserved and quiet self until that time came.

In spite of the fact that Septimus was making his best efforts to make up for his huge and utterly mortifying outburst yesterday, Amelia could not bring herself to become happy or enthusiastic about anything that he was saying, or trying to show her, as they got into the car and began their long drive back to Creede Castle. Her mind wandered in and out of flashbacks from the night before, and all of the horrible feelings she felt earlier, washed over her once again as if she was experiencing them here and now. Everything he said as he made commentary the whole way home, sounded like the drone of someone babbling on a radio in the background of a crowded but silent room. She could not stay focused; it was too difficult. The walls were officially back up. All of the passion, need, and longing that she felt to be close to him was slowly fading into nothing. And she was now just focused on making it through as much of this marriage as she had to, in one piece. She wondered to herself if she should even hold onto the hope that the universe would find it in its heart, to be merciful, and make this experience as short as possible.

Perhaps, rewarding her by making her the lady of Creede Castle shortly before taking him from her, then leaving her to grow old in this wonderful place as the distinguished widow of this beast of a man would suffice. But with the way that things were currently going for her, she was unsure if she should trust the thought of hope at all, and just give in to the realization that it had truly abandoned her altogether.

"The estate really is a wonderful place," Septimus continued to try and assure her that this was not all going to be a bad deal for her. "And don't be too anxious, my darling, I called ahead and told them not to make a huge fuss. It will only be a meager introduction of one or two of the staff. Just the house managers. This will give you plenty of time to be introduced to everyone gradually and properly. So that you are not overwhelmed, and can get used to everything." Amelia only nodded slightly to show him that she was somewhat paying attention to what he was rattling on about. And she did her best to squelch the overwhelming desire she had for him to stop talking, from rising into her face. For she knew that if it could escape there, it would be that much closer to making itself known in her voice and her words. She could not risk that. This was something that she would have to save for a time when it was worth it. And right now, in a moving vehicle, was not the safest place to make these thoughts known, she thought.

As Amelia continued to focus on the winding of the road in front of them, she took notice of how it suddenly changed. Just then, Septimus said, "Close your eyes." She looked at him in a questioning manner, feeling unsure if she can trust him. For he had certainly proved himself to be quite unpredictable and untrustworthy just the night before.

"Go on, close them." He urged with a smile in his voice. Amelia let out an unenthused sigh and closed her eyes. "And don't open them until I tell you." Amelia nodded, her mouth remaining a soft, yet harsh line. Not even the slightest glimmer of a smile.

As her eyes remain closed, she could feel the sensation of the change in texture of the road, as it passed under the wheels of the vehicle; rapidly moving over the winding, snake-like, body of what she could only figure was the long driveway leading up to the house.

"Alright, open them." Septimus instructed her. She opened her eyes and was greeted by the sight of a vast and gloriously sprawling stone structure rising up out of the ground, and rapidly coming towards them. Amelia's breath was taken away as she looked upon the beautiful building in all of its glory, towering over everything in the early afternoon sun. She began to feel the drunkenness that he had described to her on their first drive, as all of the various aromas of all of the different varieties of wild flowers populating the fields around the castle, began their dance into her nostrils and lungs. Filling her head and making her feel almost magical, like she could turn into a fairy at any moment, sprout wings and fly away through the meadow, on the pleasantly scented wind. But her awe was only to be short lived, as it was suddenly cut off by the sound of Septimus grumbling angrily to himself from the driver's seat, utterly ruining her high and bringing her spirit crashing back down to earth.

"Can you believe it?! What is it with this enormous procession?" Septimus complained. Amelia looked to see as they rounded the last corner of the drive, that there was a small multitude of people all dressed in servants' clothes, and gathered in a perfect line on either side of the walkway leading into the house. There they all stood with smiling faces, eagerly awaiting the return of their master and his new wife. Amelia smiled in excitement while she continued to look at them, doing her best to take in the sight of all of their gleaming faces. She could not understand what it was that he found so wrong with all of this, they were obviously just trying to do something nice. But leave it to him to ruin anything nice that anyone tried to do for him. She would have to remind herself not to bother doing anything nice to surprise him in the future, for fear that he would just behave like a swine with pearls and trample all over it.

"I specifically told Mrs. Warren not to make such a big fuss. For god's sake, can't a person just arrive home in peace anymore?!" He continued to grumble. Amelia bristled uncomfortably in the passenger seat and hoped that he would stop soon, or that she would be so overwhelmed by meeting the staff that she would be able to disregard his existence for a while. Even if it was just for a brief time. She desperately needed a break. She wanted to tell him so badly that it was not the house or the staff that he needed to worry about, in terms of overwhelming her and making her uncomfortable.

Septimus pulled the car to an abrupt and angry stop. the force of him stomping on the brakes like some sort of utterly displeased child, caused Amelia to be jolted forward. A short, elderly man with a bit of a limp rushed over to the passenger seat with a young boy at his side. Amelia figured that the young lad was most likely a footman in training of some sort. The old man opened the door for her and smiled widely at her, causing her to be infected by his happiness, and she smiled back. The young man reached out his hand and helped her out of the car before handing her the large and lovely, fragrant, bouquet of flowers he was cradling in one arm. "For you, ma'am." He said in a small voice.

"Thank you, they are very beautiful." Amelia said as she brought the soft flora to her face and smelled them.

"Welcome to Creede Castle, Mrs. Creede." The old man greeted her. His face suddenly changed to a more serious and apologetic expression, as he saw Septimus make his way around the car and come to stand next to her, tucking his hand gruffly into the crook of her arm, and beginning to quickly guide her down the walk, into the house, not giving her a chance to greet the once smiling faces of the procession of servants that lined the small, stone paved way.

"I am so sorry, Mr. Creede, for the big to-do. You know how Mrs. Warren is about tradition and protocol. Everything has to be just so, there is no skimping on that." The poor old butler tried his best to apologize as he made his best efforts to keep up with Septimus's brisk strides. The way he hurried himself and Amelia into the house, it was almost as if there was something chasing them.

"Tradition and protocol be damned, Wilson." He declared in a huff. "When I tell someone to do something, I expect them to do it, period." Amelia could not help but feel that somehow this rule would be strictly applied to her also. They soon made it into the house, and she couldn't help but notice the vast difference between how happy and almost hopeful the place appeared on the outside, in comparison to how dreary, dark and bleak the ancient house looked and felt on the inside. It reminded her very much of the inside of a very well-preserved inner sanctum of a mausoleum. As they came through the entry way and into the main foyer, she half expected to see crypts lining the walls, rather than the sight of a large and formidable fire place, surrounded by decorative antique artifacts. Somehow, even the great sky light where the once opulent chandelier hung, now seemed sad and ominous, instead of bright and spectacular; no longer serving its purpose to cheer the place up at all.

"Welcome to Creede Castle, Mr. and Mrs. Creede." Came a voice from the corner near the stairwell of the great stairs. The stairs passed under the skylight and divided into two sections at the top, leading respectively to either wing of the house, as they did often times in these great, old houses. Septimus let go his tight and painful grip of her arm, to walk over to the small, thin lady that seemed to have appeared out of nowhere like an apparition guarding this glorified tomb; A tomb that Amelia was sure at one time resembled a home.

"What is the meaning of this, Warren? I know for a fact that I gave you strict instructions." He began to reprimand the woman.

Amelia could not take it any longer and she decided probably against her better judgement to step in. "Thank you, very much, Mrs. Warren. It was a very lovely gesture for you to organize such a welcome." Amelia interjected quickly, putting out her hand to shake the hand of the old housekeeper. "I am, Amelia. The new Mrs. Creede. But I suppose you already know that." She smiled at Mrs. Warren as warmly as she could, trying her best to overpower Septimus's bad temper with her kindness. She could hear and feel him bristle uncomfortably at her side as she did this. But she was determined to carry on and ignore him in spite of his great and obvious displeasure.

"Thank you, madam, I was only doing what tradition requires of me, nothing more. I am, Mrs. Warren, and you can be assured that I and the rest of the staff here at the castle are completely at your disposal. Whatever you should require, you have but to ask."

"Thank you, Mrs. Warren, I will certainly keep that in mind."

"Well, look, now you're best friends." Septimus commented with a disingenuous and snide smile. Amelia did her best to restrain herself from elbowing him in the stomach, however overwhelming the temptation was. She did her best to keep eye contact with Mrs. Warren, and continued to smile, hiding her own irritation and displeasure as best as she knew how.

"I have told them to lay out tea in the drawing room for you, and after you have had the chance to have some refreshment and get your bearings Mrs Creede, I will show you to your room. If that is satisfactory to you, madam?" Mrs. Warren informed her with an indication of emotion.

"That is quite to my liking, thank you once again, Mrs. Warren."

Tea went by very silently, as Amelia sat on one of the small sofas in the drawing room and Septimus could not seem to sit still. It was almost like there was something after him that would not allow him to be stationary for even a second. She however, did not feel that it would be best to ask him what the matter was, for fear that he would probably try to bite her head off once again, as he seemed so content to do with everyone else in the house just now.

After finishing her tea, she decided to track down Mrs. Warren, who was not very hard to find, and allow her to give her a tour of the house on her way to showing her to her room. Amelia was completely amazed by the vast expanse of this grand structure that seemed to go on forever and ever, without any kind of end in sight. Even the ceilings gave the impression that their reach was nearly infinite, as they vaulted seemingly into the heavens, far above Amelia's head. They made her already small frame feel just that much smaller in the grand scheme of things and she found herself pausing many times during their walk through the house and up the stairs, past the galleried hall that she had heard so much about, which was dressed with many paintings and portraits of various people and scenes. Amelia looked intently and eagerly into each of their faces, wondering who they were and what their history was concerning the house. But she did not want to bog Mrs. Warren down with too many questions, or give her the impression that she was just a silly child. So, she refrained and did her best to perceive the possible answers herself. Which she felt was in a way more fun anyhow. Just enjoying the sensation of all the history and legend that saturated the walls of this place. There was an obvious presence that lingered here, that hung in the air. She couldn't quite put her finger on it, she guessed that it most likely was something that the staff would attribute to the resident house spirit, as most people in their station were very big on omens and portends. She only hoped that she would never do anything to offend the house spirit.

Amelia stood there for what she thought was only a moment, looking into the eyes of a woman's portrait that hung in the gallery at the top of the stairs. But when she turned, she noticed that Mrs. Warren was waiting there for her quite patiently, and she suddenly felt quite uncomfortable at the realization that she had most likely kept this poor woman waiting a lot longer than she believed.

"Oh, Mrs. Warren, I am so terribly sorry. I had no intention of keeping you waiting. I didn't mean to slow you down, so." Amelia apologized profusely, feeling quite embarrassed of herself.

"There is no need for you to apologize, madam. You can take as long as you please. My time is yours now, ma'am." Mrs. Warren replied.

Amelia followed her over the top landing and down the narrow hallway to a small room. It was very bright and cheery looking. Like something someone would see if they imagined a little girl's room. It was a vision of bright pinks and spritely yellows. And there seemed to be no end to the ruffles and lace, when it came to the bed clothes and the canopy that draped over the top of the four posts, towering over the narrow, single bed. This struck Amelia as slightly odd, as she thought that since Septimus and she were now husband and wife, they would be sharing a room. And this bed was certainly not big enough for the both of them to sleep in, much less fit in comfortably. Amelia remembered what Septimus had told her about the view from the windows, and she began to get excited once again, as she made her way over to the window seat that sat nestled between two great bay windows. Pulling the curtains back with the anticipation of seeing the sea, she found herself suddenly disappointed, as she did not find that to be the view from her window at all. But instead, it was a view of a small patch of garden near the front of the house.

"I thought that you could see the sea from the windows. How come I cannot see it from mine?" Amelia asked Mrs. Warren.

"That is because that is the view from the master bedroom, which is in the west wing of the house. Mr. Creede had everything moved from there to the east wing, because no one goes in there anymore."

"Oh, I see. Isn't that very odd though? we are husband and wife, and we will not be rooming together?"

"You will find in these circles, with the old families, that it is the usual custom. Except of course, for the former Lady Creede. She would have none of that. When she was alive, they both lived in the most beautiful room of the house, overlooking the sea."

Amelia tried to quash the feeling that Mrs. Warren was trying to rub it in that somehow, she was not good enough to get the better room. But she had only just met this woman, there was no reason for her to harbor any ill will towards her. So, thoughts that Mrs. Warren would have a motive to do such things could only be utter nonsense. She could not let the lens with which Septimus had colored everything, ruin her own personal view of everyone. They were surely not all like him.

"If that's the case, I shall do my best to become accustomed to everything as it should be. I really do hope that the two of us can really become friends, Mrs. Warren. I hope that we can begin to truly understand one another. And make Septimus happy, of course."

"Of course, madam. I will do everything in my power to make sure that your stay is satisfactory." responded Mrs. Warren. As Amelia watched the old woman turn and begin to make her way out of the narrow doorway leading into the hall, she got the sudden feeling that what Mrs. Warren had said made it sound like she, Amelia, would be there only for a short time. "My stay?" She repeated the words silently to herself. But she quickly brushed off the thought, once again telling herself that she was just being silly and paranoid. It was just the fact that she was in a new place, and she had not gotten the chance to truly settle in and make it her own yet. She was sure that once she had the opportunity to spend a few nights there, she would no longer have these bouts of fear and doubt, about people like Mrs. Warren wishing bad things on her anymore.

Mrs. Warren paused in the doorway for a moment and turned to face Amelia once again. "I apologize, madam, but it nearly slipped my mind to ask you."

"What is it, Mrs. Warren?"

"I needed to ask you when your maid will be arriving?"

"My maid? Oh my. I'm afraid that I don't have one of my own." Amelia started to experience that feeling of being inadequate and out of place which she knew so very well.

"Would you like one, madam? It is usually customary for the lady of the house to have her own personal maid."

"I am terribly sorry Mrs. Warren, I understand. You will have to be patient with me as I endeavor to learn all of these sorts of things. I trust that if you believe it to be best that I have one, then by all means I shall hire one. But I would certainly hate to cause any disruptions to how you run the house or the staff. So, if you would like to hire one for me, I trust your judgement completely. Perhaps, some young girl from the village looking to train. Or one of the tweens looking to move up. Whatever you think is best."

"As you wish, madam." Mrs. Warren nodded and departed the room.

"Thank you, Mrs. Warren." Amelia called after her quietly.

******

Just as brightly as the sun had shone through the curtains and poured into Amelia's new living quarters, the darkness was thick and nearly blinding. Its silent yet obvious nature seemed to hum in the quiet unquiet of Amelia's mind, with its own almost audible voice that whispered to her how she did not belong here. She lay there in the small, narrow bed that was entirely too firm for her taste, reminding her very much of one of those purgatorial hospital cots that she would catch a few winks on, when she volunteered as a nurse during the war. She tried with all of her might to tuck herself into her covers as tightly as possible, and close her eyes, hoping that at some point she would just become too exhausted to fight the sleep that would inevitably come, and would just pass out. But she found instead that she was just waiting in frustrating agony. The minutes whirred past her like eternal hours, refusing to bring her the sleep she so desperately desired. Since she was a child, Amelia had never liked the sensation of sleeping alone. It was so cold and separate. Even though during the day, in her waking hours, she found that she did not mind the idea of long periods of time spent in solitude. But at night, she needed to feel close to someone. She needed the comfort of knowing that she was not the only one in the world. Amelia had believed that since she was now a married woman, this was a sensation that she would never have to fear experiencing ever again. But like most things in her life just now, she found herself to be quite mistaken. For here she was, laying here in this cold and lonely room, completely on her own. Or was she?

As time continued to pass in this dark and seemingly empty tomblike place, she began to get the sneaking suspicion that somehow, she was not completely by herself in this room. This same feeling, she had felt it upon coming into the house, and it had crept over her again. Its cold, wet, fingers walking its way over her now moistening skin, causing all of the hair on the back of her neck to stand at attention. A flood of goose pimples rushed all over the rest of her body, scratching against the silk of her night dress, and heightening the sensation that much more. This presence was not one that comforted her by its sudden appearance. It was dark and foreboding. She likened herself to someone who finds themselves shipwrecked at night in the dark waters of the ocean, unable to see the hungry predators that swim beneath the surface, but still overwhelmed by the knowledge that they were there waiting to consume her.

Amelia did her best to convince herself that she was tired. This was all just a trick that her mind was trying to play on her, in the midst of her emotional turmoil and exhaustion. Everything would look better in the morning if she could only just get some rest. She closed her eyes tightly once again, pulling the covers over her head to deepen the darkness around her, when suddenly, as sure as she was surrounded by only the sound of her own labored breathing, she heard it. The creak of the wood paneling on the floor, the scrape of fabric from what she could only imagine was a long skirt, trailing across the rug that lay next to her bed. Her eyes popped open and stared into the deep blackness under her comforter. She searched her mind in wide eyed, lidless fear for thoughts on what to do. Should she dare run? The oppressive feeling of someone standing over her grew more and more, as her terror reached a boiling point. Amelia ripped the covers down from her face, trembling in anticipation of the image that rushed into her mind. It was that of a dark silhouette of a woman with long, grasping, gray fingers, standing over her, and reaching out to take hold of her. The images behind her eyes melding with the empty reality in her room, caused her to see the tall, ominous figure of a woman traced in the bright moonlight. Her long, dark, wet hair hanging over her face, and sticking to her nightgown. The gown in turn, clinging to her body and revealing every curve of her womanly form.

"Persephone," Amelia felt the breath pass over her lips as she believed she whispered the name to herself, but it did not sound like her own voice, and instead of hearing it come from her own mouth; the breath of the name tickled at her ear. And the cold, clay like, touch of fleshy lips brushed against the skin of her earlobe. But she was too afraid to shutter, afraid to shrink away from it for fear that somehow, this specter would carry her away into the night to be drowned in the sea as she had been.

Amelia sat there frozen in her terror, closing her eyes once again and praying in frantic whispers to herself, that the image and the presence would leave her just as quickly as they had arrived. The feeling slowly began to pass away, as she heard the chime of the clock down the hall ring out four o'clock. The witching hour was officially over. Despite the fact that she had never really been one to believe in such superstitions as the dead being able to walk the earth during the three o'clock hour, it was as if this place had changed all of that for her too. She didn't know what to believe anymore. The lines between reality and fantasy were all but blurred to her now, and there was no way for her to calm herself as she had done so many times before, with the consoling thought that it was all in her head. Because now, she couldn't be completely sure.

Amelia dug deep within herself, mustering the strength to move past her overriding terror and fling herself out of the bed, nearly tossing her small body onto the hard, unforgiving wood of the floor beneath her. She gathered herself to a wobbly but standing position. Straightening her night gown, she did not bother to retrieve her dressing gown from the end of the bed, she was in too much of a hurry. She needed to get out of there. Rushing to the door, she flung it open and tore down the long, narrow, dark hallway, not even closing the door to her own bedroom behind her. Her eyes dove in and out of all of the many open doors that lined the passageway, in her passionate and frantic search for Septimus's room. She could not care for the fact that he had been so beastly to her and everyone else of late. She could not stand to be alone any longer, not like this. Desperate times certainly called for desperate measures here, and she was certainly in a great state of desperation; feeling that at any moment she would certainly go mad and run from the house, screaming like some sort of banshee.

Finally, Amelia came to a closed door at the far end of the hallway. She hoped that her assumption was correct in believing this to be his room. If it wasn't, she was in for a rude surprise, but she was certain that it surely could not be any worse than the great shock that she had just experienced in her own room. She reached out a trembling hand to grasp the cold metal of the brass doorknob. Turning it slowly, she opened the door as quietly as she could. Letting herself into the room that was not quite as dark as hers, she closed the door behind her carefully, and tip-toed over to the large bed that sprawled out, nearly taking up the whole middle of the room. Amelia climbed into the bed cautiously and covered herself with the comforter duvet.

Septimus stirred slightly, she turned over and lay there quietly, trying not to make any sudden movements that would wake him. Just then, she felt his strong but gentle hand take hold of her exposed arm. "What do we have here?" He asked in a half asleep, but pleasantly surprised tone. Amelia turned over slowly to look into his eyes. "I'm sorry, my darling, I was just feeling a bit lonely and frightened on my own. I hope I have not disturbed you too badly. I can go back if you like." Amelia apologized, sitting up slightly as if she were about to leave for her own room again. But she was stopped by Septimus pulling her closer to himself. Leaning over her, he placed a soft and fervent kiss on her lips, telling her everything she needed to know. He had no desire for her to leave him. And, she felt that his telling of this to her, meant more than just not leaving his bed. She could sense his great fear that somehow, his behavior had given rise to her desire to depart from there and return to her previous life, before there was any memory of him. Leading her to forget him all together.

Amelia reciprocated his affections, pressing her own small frame into his, encouraging his grasping and massaging fingers to wander her body as she continued to kiss him fervently. Allowing her mind to be completely consumed by the high of her aching and yearning body, letting the rest of the world fall away, and forgetting that there was anything else in existence on earth; except what she desired so deeply, his undying love for her.

Chapter 8

Septimus awoke slowly out of his deep slumber to find small slices of young, dappled, morning sunlight, coming through the cracks in between the thick, dark curtains that covered the vast windows of his bedroom. A bit of cool air from the draftiness of the old house brushed over his bare skin, yet he still was comforted by the warmth of the still heated body lying next to him. He lay there for another moment, quietly observing the peacefully sleeping naked form of his beautiful, young wife. She looked so angelic and innocent as she slept. He wondered what sort of dreams were passing behind her gently closed eyes, that were delightfully bordered by long eye lashes that barely graced the top of her small, rounded cheeks. Septimus gently swept the stray locks of her now short, golden hair away from her face, so that he could take on the full view of her sweet face. So pale, so perfect, like a porcelain doll. She reminded him almost of a slumbering forest nymph in deep repose, waiting for spring to come forth and give her the kiss of life that she so desperately wanted. Awakening her wide eyed and wonderful self to the bright new world that offered itself willingly to her love. He only wished that he could be so open with her, the way that everything else in the world around them seemed to be so generous with her. He supposed this was because she was such a generous and loving person, and that was why everything desired to offer itself to her. For what you give you get back, and he had certainly been very stingy. Septimus mentally chastised himself and felt the pain of the whips on his back, as he lay back and covered his eyes with his large, sprawling hand.

He should never have brought her here, he thought to himself. This was his first mistake. He should have listened to the voice of reason that tried to relay the warnings to him in all of her reservations. His mind went back to that first magical night they spent together in Venice. Septimus remembered how her eyes sparkled, and all of her seemed to shine with innocent and unabashed wonder the whole time they were there. Even though he was not much for being a romantic, he found that when he was with her, he wanted to do all of the things that young lovers would do. She needed to know what it was like to sail through the streets of Venice hand in hand, in a gondola, with a man who worshipped her wholly. And he found that he was completely at her mercy, not denying her anything that she wanted.

Like waves of the ocean outside crashing onto the shore, the images and feelings of that night came flooding back to him. He remembered how desperate he was to have her, to feel himself inside her. He wanted to consume her with the fire of his raging passion. Septimus groaned to himself as he recalled the warmth of her soft, alabaster skin under his fingers, and the taste of her perfect, welcoming breasts on his tongue, as he kissed and suckled her like a man who had been starved for centuries of not only food, but the touch of another human being. Her cries and moans resounding in his ears like something out of a far-off dream, her entire body trembling with enraptured pleasure, as she closed her eyes and clawed at his skin. Her soul begging him to keep going and never stop.

While they lay there, he combed his fingers through her sweat moistened hair, and smiled down on her gleaming satisfied face. He felt that the incandescent glow that exuded from her was not only from the small jewels of sweat that dappled her face, but from her own happiness. The happiness that his love had afforded her. And, he would be more than willing to do whatever it took to keep her looking this pleased. But suddenly, her face changed as he watched the silent thoughts pass like swimming sharks behind her eyes. The predators of doubt that he wished more than anything to vanquish for her.

"A penny for your thoughts" he said thoughtfully. "I don't have one on me, so I suppose a kiss will have to do instead." Septimus kissed her softly. Amelia laughed quietly, but he could hear the sound of sadness and pain behind the low hum of her chuckle. "What is it, my darling?" He lifted her chin, causing her to have to look into his searching eyes, as he tried to decipher her thoughts before she could utter a word.

"Did I make the right decision? Doing this I mean, marrying you." Amelia asked with a look of sadness and the need for confirmation in her eyes.

"Why would you ask such a thing?" His heart dropped and he felt the grip of panic in his throat nearly catching his words.

"It's just that we may have rushed into this before considering if I was right for you. If I was right for your world. You and I come from different places. And, I would hate for people to think any lesser of you by seeing how out of place I am at your side." She worried.

"What of my world? Allow me to be the judge of what I think fits and what doesn't, alright..." the sound of his voice in his memory trailed off, as he returned his gaze to the sleeping angel beside him.

Septimus scolded himself once again for not listening. It was not the fact that it was a mistake to marry her at all. It was the fact that he had been so selfish in thinking that somehow, they could actually be happy here in this place. This horrid yet wonderful place. The last bastion of all of the memories he wished he could just wipe away, but found it nearly impossible. This is why he needed her here. He coveted her light and hoped that by the brightness of her soul, all of the shadows that haunted him here in this glorified tomb would be chased away, never to return again. But he was ruining that, squelching her light with the great blistering wind of his unmanageable character. For really, the problem lay with him, not this place. But he would not dare to admit that, except in the lonely, quiet corners of his mind where he often found himself trapped by all of the voices that told him this was all his fault. He was the one responsible for everyone's unhappiness.

Persephone, the voices belonged to her. Just as everything here seemed to still belong to her, held tightly in her cold, harsh grasp as it always had been. Even he himself was still under her thumb somehow. Despite the fact that she had been long dead, she had still found a way to manipulate things to her liking. She would never be at peace until he was utterly ruined and miserable, just as when she was alive. And somehow, in death, he still could not escape her wishes.

Completely overwhelmed now by all of these clamoring thoughts, he needed desperately to clear his head. He needed to go for a walk about the grounds and allow the drunkenness of the aroma, and beauty of the place wash away his misery. So, he gathered himself from the bed and set off to find his peace. The best he could hope for today was to keep his focus on the fact that he was no longer alone, and he must now endeavor to do better. And, no longer behave in such a way that would ultimately drive her away. For that would certainly and irrevocably destroy him.

*****

Amelia stood in the middle of the vast foyer of the house, the light pouring down on her from the skylight like a harsh spotlight. The chandelier hanging and swaying precariously over her head like it could fall at any moment. She slowly crept her way up the stairs on the way up to her room. Making it up to the middle landing, she looked over to her left and noticed that the door to the west wing was sitting slightly open. Stopping for a moment and looking around to see if there was anyone walking through the house, she saw that she was completely alone. There was no one to see her if she were to slip quietly into the doorway. Her curiosity got the better of her and she cautiously walked up the small flight of steps leading to the open door that opened even further, without her needing to touch it even slightly. It stood there agape, the long, dark passageway behind it stretching far, yet close somehow. She stalked into the corridor and walked quietly through, looking side to side into the alternating closed and open rooms that lined either side of the hallway. Each room appearing as if they were all well preserved shrines to people who had once dwelt in them. But it was quite obvious from all of the dust and cobwebs that lined the windows, that no one had been in this part of the house for quite some time. The sound of a large, oak door opening and closing resounded through the vaulted passage, and caught her attention, drawing her focus irreversibly to the room that lay at the end of the hallway. She stood there for a moment, staring at the closed door. The end of the hallway seemed to draw itself closer to her, though she stood there completely still and stationary. Her sight honing in on it, like it was now the only thing there with her. It called to her silently with a siren's voice that pulled at her insides, beckoning her to come closer, and inviting her in. She moved forward, involuntarily drawn to it as if she was being pulled forward by some magnetic force, causing her to almost levitate; for she could not feel the sensation of her own footsteps as she came closer. Then, suddenly, there it was in front of her. Amelia reached out for the doorknob, but did not even feel herself touch it or turn the knob, and the door opened as the other one had before. She floated silently into the room that was covered with the most unquiet silence she had ever heard. The same feeling she had experienced when she first entered the house came over her once again. The cold presence of that which was long dead, passed over her, and made her shutter as it crawled over and into her skin like a thousand tiny spiders made of ice and fire.

The sound of breath behind her and the sense of another presence other than herself coming into the room, fell upon her suddenly. The scent of decaying flesh and seaweed assaulted her nostrils and burned her eyes. She stood there in frozen terror believing that if she did not turn around, the figure that stood behind her would cease to exist somehow. But no matter how hard she closed her eyes, the presence seemed to grow rather than diminish.

Just then the bedroom door leading out into the hallway, her only exit, slammed shut, and she heard the bolt fasten tightly. She overflowed with panic as she knew now that her only way of escape had been cut off. The long, spindly fingers of her captor grasped her fragile shoulders, the woman's long, talon like nails dug painfully into her skin. Spinning her around to look into her eyes, Amelia raised her hands over her face and cried out in a loud, resounding shriek.

The pierce of her cries rang through her ears, causing her to wake suddenly out of her heavy slumber. Her body screamed with pain, as though she had been violently thrown from a state of deep sleep paralysis into waking reality. The blood that rushed from her head to the rest of her limbs seemed as if it were on fire, causing every nerve in her body to twitch in rebellion and terror, against its feverish rampage. She tilted her swimming head slightly to the right and realized that she need not fear disturbing her sleeping husband, for it was now morning, and he was no longer in bed beside her.

She was soon comforted by the sensation of warmth, making its way to her skin through the annoying draft that passed through the windows, and she smiled, upon realizing that a small fire had been made in the fireplace nestled carefully in the wall, a short distance from the bed. The curtains had also been drawn back, allowing the full light of the mid-morning sun to shine through the sparkling panes, adding a glow and warmth to the room as well. For once she had been right, things did look better by the light of day. Perhaps this was a sign that things were not going to be so bad after all, she thought. Until she looked down at herself and suddenly began to feel slightly embarrassed at the revelation that she had been lying there stark naked, without even the comforter over her, and one of these poor servants had come in here to draw the curtains and light the fire. Oh, dear. What a shock that would have been for someone. She only hoped that it was not the poor butler Mr. Wilson, or god forbid Mrs. Warren. She already felt uncomfortable and ashamed around her enough, without the idea that this woman has now seen all there was to see of her. Now nothing could be left to anyone's imagination at all now, could it? Amelia could only imagine what sort of a girl they thought she believed herself to be, sleeping in so late and lying there completely nude. This was certainly not the behavior of a lady of the manor.

With this in mind, she quickly got up, retrieving her nightgown from the floor. Putting it on hastily, she made her way to her room as fast as she was able, and got dressed to go down to breakfast. She could not believe that this was the impression she was going to give everyone in the house of her. First day here and she is late to breakfast. Amelia chastised herself the entire way down stairs and into the dining room, where she found that no one seemed to care that she was late. This was some consolation. Wilson smiled at her kindly and wished her good morning as he poured her tea and brought her an egg and some toast. Being sure to let her know that the butter was fresh, and they had brought up a fresh jar of marmalade for her, because they had been told it was to her liking. All seemed right with the world once again. And there was Septimus, the perfect picture of an English gentleman, sitting across from her, engrossed in his morning paper, and drinking his tea. He smiled at her over the top of his paper as he turned the page.

"Good morning, my darling. Did you sleep well?" He inquired in a kind and cheerful, but dry voice.

Amelia thought for a moment about her nightmare, debating with herself if she should bother him with it by telling him in fact that she had not slept well the entire night. But this was not something that she felt was necessary. From the stack of open mail, to the side of his half-eaten breakfast plate, she could see that surely there were far more important things he needed to concern himself with, than whether she had a little bad dream or not. "Yes, I did, thank you. And you? my love"

"For the most part, yes. I took a bit of an early walk this morning. I hope I didn't disturb you; Marnie can be so very loud at times."

"Marnie?" She asked confused.

"Oh, yes, my house dog. That's right, my dear, you haven't met him yet. Don't worry you will soon enough, he's always wandering about here somewhere. Usually getting into some kind of trouble." He smiled and went back to his paper.

Amelia turned her attention to the soft-boiled egg in front of her before suddenly having a thought. "Septimus?"

"Yes, dear one."

"The portrait of that woman in the gallery,"

"Mhmm?"

"Who is she?"

"She is some great aunt so and something, from so far back, there is more than one great to be said in front of her title. But she is old enough for me to be entirely too young to remember what her name is." He droned on indifferently.

UNLOCKABLES

Congrats on achieving a milestone! (getting to the end of this book). For that, you get a chance to enjoy another BadCreative book. Support your local publisher by grabbing another amazing, novel on offer
>>> here <<<US
>>> here <<< UK
>>> here <<< FR
>>> here <<< DE

>>> here <<< and >>> here <<<

You can also pledge allegiance to Castle Creede with this awesome #CastleCreede t-shirt. Only available in the US and at this price >>> here <<< and >>> here <<<

Thank you for purchasing, and don't forget to drop us a review on our Amazon page. #BewitchingAmelia